THE CHARLESTON KNIFE IS BACK IN TOWN

The Hardman Series

THE CHARLESTON KNIFE IS BACK IN TOWN

RALPH DENNIS

BRASH
BOOKS

Introduction "Ralph Dennis & Hardman"
Copyright © 2018 by Joe R. Lansdale. All Rights Reserved.

ISBN: 1-7320656-7-5
ISBN-13: 978-1-7320656-7-3

Published by
Brash Books, LLC
12120 State Line #253,
Leawood, Kansas 66209
www.brash-books.com

INTRODUCTION

Ralph Dennis and Hardman
By Joe R. Lansdale

O nce upon the time there were a lot of original paperbacks, and like the pulps before them, they covered a lot of ground. Western, adventure, romance, mystery, science fiction, fantasy, and crime, for example.

There were also subsets of certain genres. One of those was the sexy, men's action-adventure novel with a dab of crime and mystery.

These books had suggestive titles, or indicators that not only were they action packed with blood and sweat, fists and bullets, but that there would be hot, wet sex. They were straight up from the male reader's perspective, the perspective of the nineteen seventies and early eighties.

There were entire lines of adult westerns for example. They sold well at the time. Quite well. These Westerns sold so well, that for a brief period it seemed as if it might go on forever. They made up the largest number of Westerns on the stands rivaled only by Louis L'Amour, and a few reprints from Max Brand and Zane Grey.

An agent once told me I was wasting my time writing other things, and I could be part of this big stable he had writing adult Westerns. Although I had nothing against sexy Westerns, which may in fact have been pioneered as a true branch of the Western genre by a very good writer named Brian Garfield and his novel *Sliphammer*, but I didn't want to spend a career writing them. Not the sort I had read, anyway.

Still, a small part of me, the part that was struggling to pay bills, thought maybe I could write something of that nature that might be good enough to put a pen name on. Many of my friends and peers were doing it, and some actually did it quite well, but if ever there was a formulaic brand of writing, that was it.

I was a big fan of Westerns in general, however, so I thought I might could satisfy that itch, while managing to satisfy the publisher's itch, not to mention that of the Adult Western reader, primarily males.

I picked up a number of the so called adult Westerns, read them, and even landed a job as a ghost for one series, but the publisher and the writer had a falling out, so my work was never published, though I got paid.

Actually, for me, that was the best-case scenario. Once I started on the series I knew I was in for trouble. It wasn't any fun for me, and that is the main reason I write. I woke up every morning feeling ill because I was trying to write that stuff. It was like trying to wear a tux to a tractor pull.

I thought, maybe there's something I would like more in the action-adventure line, crime, that sort of thing. I had read *The Executioner*, and had even written three in the *M.I.A. Hunter* series, and frankly, next to nailing my head to a burning building, I would rather have been doing anything else. But a look at our bank account made me more pliable.

But that was later. At the time I was looking at this sort of genre, trying to understand if there was anything in it I could truly like, I picked up a book by Ralph Dennis, *The Charleston Knife is Back in Town*, bearing the overall title of *Hardman*. The books were billed by the publisher as "a great new private eye for the shockproof seventies."

The title was suggestive in a non-subtle way, and I remember sighing, and cracking it open and hoping I could at least make it a third of the way through.

And then, it had me. It gripped me and carried me through, and one thing was immediately obvious. It wasn't a sex and shoot novel. It's not that those were not components, but not in the way of the other manufactured series, where sometimes the sex scenes were actually lifted from another one in the series and placed in the new one, in the perfunctory manner you might replace a typewriter ribbon.

I was working on a typewriter in those days, and so was everyone else. If that reference throws you, look it up. You'll find it somewhere between etched stone tablets and modern PCs.

Dennis wrote with assurance, and he built characterization through spot on first person narration. His prose was muscular, swift, and highly readable. There was an echo behind it.

Jim Hardman wasn't a sexy private eye with six-pack abs and face like Adonis. He was a pudgy, okay looking guy, and as a reader, you knew who Hardman was and how he saw things, including himself, in only a few pages.

You learned about him through dialogue and action. Dennis was good at both techniques. His action was swift and realistic, and you never felt as if something had been mailed in.

Hardman wasn't always likable, or good company. And he knew that about himself. He was a guy just trying to make it from day to day in a sweltering city. He had a friend named Hump, though Hardman was reluctant to describe him as such. In his view he and Hump were associates. He sometimes hired Hump to help him with cases where two men, and a bit of muscle, were needed.

That said, Hump was obviously important to Hardman, and as the series proceeded, he was more so. The books developed their world, that hot, sticky, Atlanta landscape, and it was also obvious that Dennis knew Atlanta well, or was at least able to give you the impression he did.

His relationship with Marcy, his girlfriend, had a convenient feel, more than that of a loving relationship, and it was off again and on again; it felt real, and the thing that struck me about the books was that there was real human fabric to them. There was action, of course, but like Chandler and Hammett before him, Dennis was trying to do something different with what was thought of as throw away literature.

I'm not suggesting Dennis was in the league of those writers, but he was certainly head and shoulders above the mass of paperbacks being put out fast and dirty. When I read Dennis's Hardman novels, the characters, the background, stayed with me. The stories were peripheral in a way. Like so many of the best modern crime stories, they were about character.

Due to the publishing vehicle and the purpose of the series, at least from the publisher's view point, the books sometimes showed a hastiness that undercut the best of the work, but, damn, I loved them. I snatched them up and devoured them.

I thought I might like to do something like that, but didn't, and a few years later I wrote those *M.I.A. Hunters*, which I actually loathed, and knew all my visitations with that branch of the genre I loved, crime and suspense, had ended, and not well, at least for me, though the three books were later collected and published in a hardback edition from Subterranean Press by me and its creator, Stephen Mertz.

A few years after that journey into the valley of death, quite a few, actually, I had a contract with Bantam, and I was trying to come up with a crime novel, and I wrote about this guy named Hap standing out in a field in East Texas, and with him, out of nowhere, was a gay, black guy named Leonard.

The idea of a black and white team in the depths of East Texas would be something I could write about, and it was a way for me to touch on social issues without having to make a parade of it. I thought, yeah, that'll work for me, and though my characters are quite different than Hardman, they share many similarities as well. The black and white team and Southern background (East Texas is more South than Southwestern), was certainly inspired by the Hardman novels. I think because it rang a bell with me, the clapper of that bell slapped up against my own personal experience, though mine was more rural than urban.

Even more than other writer heroes of mine, Chandler and Chester Himes for example, Hardman spoke directly to me. Chandler's language and wise cracks fit the people I grew up with, and Himes wrote about the black experience, something that was vital to the South, though often given a sideways consideration and the back of culture's hand. But Hardman had that white blue collar feel, even if he was in the city and was already an established, if unlicensed, private investigator and thug for hire. I blended all those writers, and many more, to make Hap and Leonard, John D. McDonald, certainly, but if I had a spirit guide with the Hap and Leonard books, it was Ralph Dennis.

So now we have the Hardman books coming back into print.

I am so excited about this neglected series being brought back, put in front of readers again. It meant a lot to me back then, and it still means a lot. You can beef about the deficiency of political correctness, but twenty years from now they'll be beefing about our lack of political correctness on some subject or another that we now think we are hip to. And too much political correctness is the enemy of truth, and certainly there are times when fiction is not about pretty manners but should ring the true bells of social conditions and expression. Erasing what is really going on, even in popular fiction, doesn't do anyone any favors. Righteous political correctness has its place, but political correct police do not.

I know very little about Ralph Dennis. I know this. He wrote other books outside the Hardman series. I don't think he had the career he deserved. The Hardman books were a product of their time, but they managed to be about their time, not of it. They stand head and shoulders above so much of the paperback fodder that was designed for men to hold the book in one hand, and something else in the other. And I don't mean a can of beer.

But one thing is for sure, these books are still entertaining, and they are a fine time capsule that addresses the nature and attitudes of the time in which they were written. They do that with clean, swift prose, sharp characterization, and an air of disappointment in humanity that seems more and more well-earned.

I'm certainly glad I picked that Hardman novel up those long years ago. They were just what I needed. An approach that imbedded in my brain like a knitting needle, mixed with a variety of other influences, and helped me find my own voice. An authentic Southern voice. A voice that wasn't that of New York or Los Angeles or Chicago, but a voice of the South.

Thanks Ralph Dennis for helping me recognize that my background was as good a fodder for popular fiction as any, and that popular fiction could attempt to rise above the common crime novel. I don't know that I managed that, but Ralph Dennis was one of those writers that made me try.

Dennis may not have made literature of Hardman, but he damn sure touched on it more than a time or two, and I wish you the joy I got from first reading these novels, so many long, years ago.

Read on.

PUBLISHER'S NOTE

This book was originally published in 1974 and reflects the cultural and sexual attitudes, language, and politics of the period.

CHAPTER ONE

In the prelim bout two welterweights were going at it, a young black from Atlanta and a Cuban from New York City who had large raw patches of acne on his chest and back. Every time the black hit the Cuban on one of the splotches I'd catch myself wincing. In the seat next to me, big and black, six-seven and 270 the last time I asked, Hump Evans was facing away from the ring, not because the punches on the acne bothered him that much but because the show in the aisles was much better than the one down in the ring.

We were in the Omni, the new sports palace in Atlanta, that red-rusting, egg-carton jumble of steel that the owners assured everybody would weather into a bluish-purple beauty of a building in time. But that was the outside. Inside it reminded me of Madison Square Garden the last time I'd been there for a holiday tournament. The same seating hassle. Good seats in the low and courtside area but hell up in the nickel seats. We were in the good seats because we'd done a bit of a favor for one of the promoters a few months back and Hump had had brass enough to remind him of it. That was how we'd ended up in the $50 seats.

Hump turned around and looked at the prelim fight for a second and then grinned at me. "Hardman, you believe all this?"

I guess I did. I'd been blinking ever since we'd parked over in the lot and followed the underpass over to the Omni. We were in the middle of a massive black celebration, complete with all the far-out fashions and a carnival spirit. It had been going on for about a week and this was the high point of it all, the J.C. Cartway fight, his first since the Supreme Court had ruled for him and sprung him out of the New York pen where he'd been doing five for possession of hard drugs. The Cartway case, from the arrest through the trial and right up to the series of appeals, had seemed tailored for cause purposes. It had been a big cause, not just for the blacks but for everybody who thought the system of justice in this country could be warped at times. J.C. Cartway was probably the best young heavyweight in the country since Ali. By itself that would have been all right. What rubbed some of the Establishment wrong was that he was a Black Panther and he didn't take shit off anybody. To say the least, the arrest had the stink of a big fish-kill on the Coast. Just earlier that day Cartway had had a row with some white cops outside a bar on Sheridan Square. He wasn't doing anything. They probably stopped him because he looked prosperous and for a black that must have meant to the cops that he was a pimp or a dealer. Cartway had had enough sense not to be baited into using his fists, but he'd given them a lot of mouth. So it looked strange, not twelve hours later, when a narc squad showed up at Cartway's apartment with a search warrant. In the search, while J.C. sat in the living room drinking buttermilk, the narcs found twenty decks of H. ready for street sale. According to the cops, that made J.C. a dealer. According to J.C., the stuff had been planted on him because he wouldn't let the cops play with his balls.

The *Free J.C.* signs sprouted all over the country and it was almost a year after the heated trial before the appeals worked their way through the courts. During that time J.C. sweated in the prison laundry and worked out in the gym. He got meaner and harder and he stayed in shape. Still, he hadn't had a fight in that time and maybe he had overtrained. When he had got out of the pen four months previously, the world was waiting for his next fight. Even if he hadn't been a damned good fighter, they'd have been waiting for it.

There was, it seemed, one problem. The New York State Boxing Commission had revoked his license to fight there and it looked like they were dragging their feet about reinstating it. It might have been the Black Panther tie-in at the center of that. It was at that moment that five civil rights leaders in Atlanta put together a package and offered the Omni as the site. They pointed with pride to the fact that Ali's first fight after the long suspension had been in Atlanta, the one with Quarry. The contracts were drawn up and the opponent chosen, a fairly good white heavyweight from Texas named George Higgins. Higgins might not have fought Cartway except for the long layoff Cartway had had. The word was he thought that he might catch Cartway when he wasn't sharp and beat him. That would open the door to the big money and the chance to move up in the ratings. It was a gamble and I guess he knew it. Or maybe his manager talked him into it.

The week before the fight, Atlanta seemed to be changing right before our eyes. All the big-name blacks from show business and sports crowded the Regency and right behind them came the big-time gamblers and bookies. And in their wake came the pimps and the whores and the small-time hustlers, the fringe world people hoping to pick up some crumbs from the fat table. There'd already been more than the weekly allowance of rip-offs, muggings, and con games.

But that was outside. Here in the Omni it was a festival, all the far-out and wild fashions warring in the aisles and the newly emerging black middle class pressed armpit to armpit with the pimps and their string of whores and the hustlers with a new hustle every minute or so.

That was the parade that Hump was watching rather than the awkward welterweight match down in the ring.

"Look at all that trim," Hump said, "look at all that out-of-town sweetmeat trim."

I nodded. I thought of the racist story I heard a big tobacco farmer from North Carolina tell once. I didn't remember the whole story but the punchline had this young black field hand looking him in the eye and saying, "Cap'n, if you could be black one Saturday night you'd never want to be white again." Maybe that was the way I felt, that it would be a hell of a thing to be black and feel the celebration the way Hump did and the way that whole milling mass of people did. In fact, I felt a little out of it. I'd been getting some hard-looking screw-yous from some of the studs seated around me, like they wanted me to know that I'd helped put J.C. away and don't you forget it. It might have gone beyond that if I hadn't been so obviously with Hump. I guess he'd felt the rankness around us and he was making a big thing of being friendly. There might have been some mean studs among them, but I think they knew who he was. He hadn't been out of pro football that long. Before the knee injury he'd been with Cleveland and right up there among the best defensive ends, about as big as Bubba Smith and maybe a step or two quicker. For the last few years Hump and I had been working together and drinking together and maybe we were friends. It was hard to tell with him. The work we did was anything that came up, as long as it paid good money and didn't call for us to work eight-hour shifts. That meant most of the time it was shady stuff, pretty far off-center. The more off-center, the better the money was. Neither Hump nor I cared that much about the Sunday school and church aspects of the jobs we did. Getting by out there in the fringe world could be hard and dirty and if you stopped to think about the ethics of the whole thing you'd get your plow cleaned fast and sudden. And you could end up down on Whitehall with a flat pocket. I wasn't quite ready for that yet and I was fairly sure that Hump never would be.

"It's about time," Hump said.

Down in the ring the welterweights were through for the night. The part of the crowd that had paid attention gave the black and the Cuban a derisive hand. When the judges and the referee gave the bout to the black on points, that didn't excite anybody either. Neither of the fighters had shown much and I had the feeling that the judgment had been made on some other basis, like having less pimples on his back and chest.

The ring was empty now, waiting for the arrival of Cartway and Higgins. The aisles were still jammed and some of that blue haze of smoke rising over us had the acrid smell of grass. In fact, I'd caught the scent before from somewhere right behind us. Hump caught it too and he gave me a lazy wink.

About that time a large and prosperous black stopped out at the end of our aisle, checked his ticket stub, and then, paying no attention to the people already seated, began walking over toes and corns toward us. He was wearing what looked like about a $500 J. Press suit and the hand nearest us flashed a ring that held a diamond about as big as a walnut. I stood up to let him by and he didn't even acknowledge it. I wasn't even there to him. As he passed me, he balled up something white in one hand and dropped it carelessly on the floor between Hump's feet. Hump waited until the man had taken his seat a dozen or so spaces away and then he reached down and picked up the envelope. He smoothed it out on his knee and took out the contents. It wasn't a letter. It was an engraved invitation.

JOHN JUSTIN MARTIN INVITES YOU TO A POST-FIGHT PARTY
IN HONOR OF J. C. CARTWAY.
10:30 until
2056 Rosewood Circle

About twelve seats away the man was looking down at his ring, turning it so that it caught the light. Hump put the invitation in his jacket pocket. "I always wanted to meet J.C."

"Go then," I said.

"Crash it with me."

I shook my head. "Not sure how welcome I'd be."

"Could be a lot of trim there."

"That could get me in trouble. You know Marcy."

"I'll tell you what you missed when I see you tomorrow," Hump said.

"If I miss anything."

A roar went up then. Cartway and Higgins were coming out of the dressing rooms, stepping over the low frame that marked the outside edge of the ice area where the hockey team, the Flames, played. It was a roar of animals and it filled the Omni until I thought the roof would have to pop off. From behind me, while the roar still swelled, a black leaned forward and passed Hump a joint in his cupped hand. Hump thanked him and sucked on it a couple of times. After he passed it back, Hump leaned toward me and wasted a little of it by blowing it in my face.

The fight lasted into the sixth round. It might have ended earlier but I got the feeling that Cartway didn't want to put Higgins away too soon. He wanted to savor it, that was it. Also, though he was strong and in good shape, he hadn't had a fight in almost a year and a half and he wasn't sharp. The meanness and the anger were there and in the opening of the sixth J.C. hit the tall, blond Texan with two or three lefts and then with a right. When the right connected it sounded like somebody had dropped a watermelon from a tenth-floor window. Higgins went down and twitched and the roar grew and grew, so strong you could feel the walls and the ceiling trembling. It grew into about half-an-hour's ovation and Hump and I stayed through it. I was yelling too until I didn't have much voice left. A couple of the blacks who'd wanted to beat my ass earlier ended up slapping me on the back and welcoming me into the party.

Cartway almost got mobbed when he left the ring. It took a dozen black-jacketed Panthers to get him through the screaming, clutching mass. Cartway looked happy but he also seemed afraid of the crowd. And that seemed strange.

We'd come in Hump's car. He drove me over to his place where I'd parked mine. Before I got out he asked if I was sure I didn't want to try the party. I said I couldn't, that Marcy wouldn't understand me being that much of a sports fan while she was out of town. Hump understood that. He liked Marcy. He didn't push it again and I got into my car and headed for my house. The last I saw of Hump he was hunched over a street map of Atlanta trying to find Rosewood Circle.

By the window light, the light outside, it was still night but graying slightly. I was awake and I wasn't quite sure why. The drinks I'd had after I got home had taken the knot out of me, the one left after the excitement of the Cartway fight. So why was I awake … turning and staring at the clock on the nightstand … at 5:23 in the morning?

I heard it then, the grinding dull sound of the front door bell. I'd packed it so that I could hardly hear it when I was asleep. Now somebody seemed to be leaning on it. The question was: Who the hell was on my doorstep at 5:23 in the morning? One way to find out. I gave up on the slippers and staggered through the dark living room, hitting one chair a glancing shot that took a bone chip out of my right hip on the way, and yanked the door open.

Hump stood there, dressed as he'd been the night before at the fight, only there was a lump on his forehead about the size of a large egg. I noticed that right away because he was dabbing at it with a handkerchief that had some bloodstains on it. It wasn't much blood, about what a bad cut shaving might give out.

"Can I come in, Hardman?"

"Sure." I stepped aside to let him in and closed the door behind him. "Wash up in the bathroom. I'll make some coffee."

I put on the coffee water and got down the cups and the jar of instant. I waited for Hump, knowing he'd probably have some tale to tell about some fight he'd had over some sweetpussy girl or other. Or how some stud had picked him out just because he was so big. When the coffee was made I sat at the kitchen table and sipped mine.

Hump came in and slumped into the chair across from me. "A shitty thing happened to me on the way to the party for J.C. Cartway."

"Tell me about it."

"J.C. didn't show, but I got taken for about seven hundred I was carrying." He shook his head. "Jim, you wouldn't believe what went on over there."

"Try me," I said.

"You won't believe it."

I grinned at him for making such a story out of it, for laying the suspense on so heavy. I got up and went over to the whiskey cabinet. I got out a new bottle of Cusenier calvados I'd bought a few days before because Marcy had been curious about it a few weeks earlier. It was supposed to be a welcome-back present. I peeled the foil off and got down a couple of juice glasses. Back at the table I poured me a light shot and one for Hump that was more a handful than anything to do with fingers. I looked at the kitchen clock Marcy had given me last Christmas and waited. He'd tell it his own way and it didn't matter to him that the minute hand was making a run for six o'clock. And because I liked the big bastard, I tipped the bottle again and gave myself another half shot and tried to shake the warm sleep out of my head.

Hump looked at the wadded-up handkerchief and made a toss for the trash can. He missed it by a couple of feet. I just grinned at him and didn't move.

"This the best crystal you got for drinking this fancy stuff?"

"It's not that fancy," I said. "I heard somewhere that back in War Number Two they used to burn it in cars." I took a sip and let it roll on my tongue. He gulped on his and washed it down with some of the coffee.

"Hardman, you wouldn't believe the smart-assed rip-off going on over there."

"Like I said, try me."

"I'd give one ball to have thought it up myself," Hump said.

"Come on," I said, mock-irritated, "that's enough promotion. Bring on the movie."

"It happened like this," Hump said. ...

After I left him the night before he'd found Rosewood Circle on the street map and headed out Peachtree to Ponce de Leon toward Decatur. That part of Decatur seemed like a hell of a place to hold a black party, but maybe the neighborhood was going downhill. Not his problem anyway. Just so there was a party when he got there. On impulse he stopped at Green's and fought the eleven-thirty crowd to buy himself a bottle of J&B. That was private stock, to be left in the glove compartment with a couple of plastic cups. In case there was some trim that took a liking to him and wanted to go out for some fresh air and a long conversation about art and literature.

It was a fairly long drive out to Decatur and it was almost midnight when he left Ponce de Leon and found himself in one of those neighborhoods where the homes had cost $150,000 twenty years ago. No way to know what they were worth now. Not that many got bought and sold these days. Just when he'd begun to think that he'd taken the wrong turn-off, he found Rosewood Circle.

It was shaped like a small horseshoe that had the ends bent in slightly. And though the Circle covered about a city block, there weren't but five houses on it. There were two houses on each side and one at the center of the closed end. All the houses were set back far from the road, hidden by walls and the natural barrier of trees. One tour of the circle convinced Hump that the party was being held at the large brick English-manor type house at the closed end of the horseshoe. They weren't very big on house numbers out there and he finally made his guess on the basis of the driveway packed bumper to tail with big, expensive cars.

Parking space was hard to find close to the house and finally Hump gave up the search and wedged in behind an LTD. All he could hope was that the owner wasn't in any great hurry to leave. It wouldn't do him much good if he was. Unless the LTD had a hidden set of wings. Outside the car he could feel the sharpness of the night air and across his body the vibrations of the bass, all that was left of the music after it filtered through the brick and the drawn drapes and curtains.

Oh, that was a time walking up the driveway. Feeling his jolly coming on, anticipating the class of trim and sweetmeat girls who'd be there just waiting for him to enter. He reached the lighted porch. After straightening his tie and dusting off his shoes with the handkerchief from his hip pocket, he rubbed a big smile onto his face and grabbed the doorknob and went inside.

Hump drained the last of the calvados and slid the glass across the table toward me. "Must have ruined some good car engines in its time."

I tipped the bottle and poured another shot for him. I'd been watching his eyes and he looked a bit woozy. He was something of a hard-ass so it must have taken quite a tap on the head to slow him down enough so they could empty his pocket. I'd seen him handle a couple of dudes without breaking much of a sweat.

"Go on with your story," I said, "before you pass out and I have to make up the rest of it for you."

"Welcome to the party." That was what Hump heard as soon as he walked through the front door. It was said to him by a man wearing a ski mask and gloves. In one hand he carried a walkie-talkie and in the other a .45 automatic, hammer back, that he'd lined up on the center of Hump's nose.

CHAPTER TWO

"**N**ot even *hands up* or anything like that?" I asked.

"Maybe they didn't see the same cowboy movies we saw," Hump said.

❧ ❧ ❧

Hump wasn't about to argue with the .45, but, just in case, right next to the man with the automatic was another man, dressed the same way, pointing a sawed-off shotgun at Hump's belly button.

"I'm not sure this is the right party," Hump said. "Maybe I'm expected at the one next door."

The two men didn't show that they'd even heard him. "Anybody else expected?" the one with the shotgun asked.

"Lights down the road, but not close yet."

The man with the shotgun wagged it at Hump. "This way." He pointed toward a wide entranceway to a room beyond the hallway. "You might as well join the other guests."

The walkie-talkie crackled and the one with the .45 put it to his ear. "Yeah, yeah," he said. Then he called to the guy with the shotgun: "More guests on the way, looking for parking now."

The shotgun edged a little close to him as they stepped through the entranceway and Hump considered it but the music hit him a lick then and he looked up and saw three other men in the center of the huge living room. All masked, all wearing guns in their waistbands. They were working through a great pile of clothing and coats and purses. It looked like a storeroom at Goodwill, but the coats were mink and leopard and the clothes didn't need the tags to show that they'd cost high money. They were sorting, putting the women's coats into huge laundry bags and the money and jewelry into a large black suitcase. From the look Hump got of the take in the suitcase they'd been at their work for quite some time.

"Strip to your shorts," the man with the shotgun said. One of the other three left the sorting pile and came over to stand next to Hump. On the way he'd taken out a short barrel S and W .38.

"Come on, Superspade, do what the man told you to."

The odds and the hardware were all wrong, Hump decided. No use wasting an effort. He kicked off his alligator loafers and dropped first his raincoat and then his suit coat into a pile. While he skinned his trousers and tossed his shirt and tie into the same jumble, one of the other two came over and began raking through the raincoat and suit coat pockets. As soon as the trousers hit the pile, that man threw the coats aside and clawed down into the pockets until he came up with Hump's roll. Unlike the man at the door and the man with the shotgun, he seemed to be wearing the thin rubber gloves, the kind women wash dishes in. He tossed the money clip aside and fanned out the bills from Hump's roll.

"Thin," he said, looking at Hump.

"It's not thin to me," Hump said. "Give it back and I'll be glad to walk out of here."

"Not from this party," the shotgun man said. "Nobody leaves this party early."

"You talk too much," the one with the stub S and W .38 said.

"Fuck you, too," the one with the shotgun said.

But the voices didn't seem hard to Hump. They seemed to be pretty young, especially the one with the shotgun. The profanity didn't quite come off. More like a studied reflex from a high-school kid who'd just learned to talk hard and couldn't quite pull it off. That stunned Hump and gave him a second thought about the shotgun when he'd had a try at it. But all that shot to hell now. Too many guns.

"Wrap this one up," the shotgun man said. "More company on the way." He moved away, back to the front door. The final man in the living room, the one who'd been bagging women's coats, straightened up and got a roll of two-inch adhesive tape from the arm of a stuffed chair. He kept his distance, making a wide circle around Hump while the stub .38 remained lined up.

"Hands behind you. Wrists together."

Hump went along with it. The man pressed his wrists together and wrapped them quickly and expertly. From the piles of clothing around the room, Hump decided he'd probably had a lot of practice. Behind him Hump heard the tape tear again and the man moved around him and planted about a six-inch strip over Hump's mouth. It was a sloppy job and the edges ran into Hump's sideburns. It was going to be hell to take off later. If he got the chance to take it off. There was always the chance that wherever the others had been taken was a bloodbath by now.

"This way," the one with the .38 said. He turned Hump by the elbow and pushed Hump ahead. There was an entranceway into a narrow hall at the right rear of the living room. The man remained behind him a pace or two as they passed closed doors on both sides and approached a closed door that dead-ended the hall. Just before he reached the door, Hump felt himself jerked around. His head was pressed against the wall. His legs were pulled back but still held together. It was like the spread cops made you do on a frisk, only Hump's hands were behind his back and he had to cramp his toes to keep his stocking feet from slipping on the waxed floor. The man behind him then taped his ankles together and jerked him upright.

"Now, be a good little bunny and hop into the room when I tell you to." He turned Hump toward the closed door and still holding his elbow, turned the knob and swung the door open. There was darkness ahead of him and for the first time Hump heard the wheezing and grunting and the sound of flesh slapping together.

"Hop now," the man said.

He'd barely reached the entranceway when the man behind him laughed and gave him a shove. He fell forward, sprawling into the massed and piled bodies. He hit people and he hit the carpet and he heard the wind go out of someone he hit with a knee and then the bodies were giving, moving away from him, making room.

Hump yawned and rubbed his mouth. "That crap went on for hours and hours. It seemed like years. Dumping men and women into the pile, coming back with others. It's a wonder somebody didn't get caught in the bottom and get busted all to hell. I guess what saved some lives is that the goddamn game room or whatever it was must have been about as big as a Canadian football field."

"That knot on your head?" I said. "You get that from somebody's elbow or knee?"

Hump opened his mouth to answer and then slapped his hand over his mouth and made a run for the kitchen sink. I braced him there until it passed and he'd emptied out. Then, while he was in the bathroom washing up and trying my brand of mouthwash, I got out the jug of all-purpose cleaner and worked on the sink.

By the time I'd given it up, Hump came back and stood in the doorway looking like a lot of the iron had gone out of him. I guess that was when I understood it. It was that hard-assed pride of his. He'd been done in and almost finished before he reached my place, but he'd be damned if he'd admit it. If he was going to get my help, it wasn't because he'd asked for it. Not even me and I guess I was his best friend and drinking buddy in the world. Of course, I might be wrong about that.

Before I left the sink I cracked the window above it an inch or so to let in some of the chill November morning air. That didn't help much with the vomit smell. Instead of that, now I had the rank urine scent of a rotting old fig tree outside. So, not better, but different.

I got Hump by the arm and turned him toward the bedroom. He saw what I was doing and kept saying that the sofa was fine. "I don't want your bed."

"I'm awake," I told him. "You're the second shift and if any of the black rubs off on the sheets I can always add bleach at the laundromat."

"Shit. ..."

But the protest went out of him and I helped him strip down to his underwear and I rolled him into the bed. I pulled the covers up around him and went into the bathroom and got a roll of gauze and a few scraps of adhesive tape. I didn't mind the black rubbing off but I didn't want to have to explain blood on the linen to Marcy. While I shaped up a bandage his eyes were closed but he wasn't asleep.

"You still want to know how I got this hickey on my head?"

"If you can make it short," I said.

"You know me, Hardman, and this is the part you're really going to believe," Hump said.

It was like being a worm in a large bucket of worms and every few minutes somebody'd throw in another handful. In time Hump worked his way around into a comer of the room. If it was going to last all night, he decided that it might be better to try to find a place away from the action and try to sleep if he could. To get to that corner he'd had to crawl over and push aside a few pissed people and just when he'd almost made it, it happened very suddenly. At about the same moment he got a whiff of expensive perfume... and his lower body seemed sucked forward until it fitted like a glove, his belly to her back, against the hard, rounded rear end of a girl.

⚜ ⚜ ⚜

"Too bad about that," I said. I fitted the crude bandage over the lump with as little pressure as I had to use.

"That's the half of it," Hump said. "You heard me talk about the bad moments that animal of mine gives me now and then? Well, this was one of them. He just couldn't seem to understand why I wasn't doing something about that girl. I kept trying to talk him down and he wasn't listening much. Like a snake on a hot day he felt the heat and he came crawling out."

"How'd the girl feel about that?"

"Huffy at first. Like she was shocked or something. Then it must have got to her and we spent a lot of time just making a crease in her silky underwear and not getting much of anywhere. I think we could have if she'd been really sure that was what she wanted. Maybe not."

"Get back to how you got the lump on your head."

"That was how," Hump said.

Not much later, while Hump was devoting all his energy and thought to trying to find a way of getting past that thin wisp of underwear, a pair of unlikely rescuers arrived. If Hump had been paying attention he'd have noticed that the door hadn't opened for some time, that no new victims had been added to the room. But he couldn't be blamed for not noticing.

Two minor hangers-on, fringe racket blacks, got an invitation by mistake and by the time they'd borrowed a car and found Rosewood Circle they'd missed the party and the chance to be robbed of the thirty-odd dollars they had between them. Along with them, in their wake, was a police patrol car that had been following them for a mile or so and wondered what two blacks in a 1955 Chevy were doing turning into that residential area. Otherwise, given a choice, it was very unlikely that anyone would have called the police.

The lights went on and the two small-timers blinked at what they'd uncovered. Hump, turning and rolling away from the girl and trying to hide that animal, had his first look at the other people who'd shared the time with him. He saw several of the biggest gamblers in the country and those were just the ones that he recognized.

"It was a riot. All those dudes and their women, half-dressed, rooting around in the piles of clothing and the women scream-ing and crying when they realized they'd lost their minks or leopards and the police were trying to find out what the hell was going on. And the police had called some more cops and sud-denly the grounds and the house were swarming with cops."

"Back to the lump," I said.

"That was when it happened. I sort of kept my eye on the girl while they were taking the tape off so I'd know her later." He reached up and doubled the pillow behind his head. "Now, Lord, that was sweetmeat hide. Five-ten, all the right hard and soft places. Just prime pelt. So I did it cool and marked time. We were in the living room and I'd found everything but my tie. I got dressed and I just strolled over to her, shaking the wrinkles out of my pants as I went."

She was standing there, skin like creamed coffee, looking sad. She had a blouse in one hand and one of those heavy sort of platform shoes in the other. Not having a ready good line for such a situation, Hump decided that he'd do the obvious.

"Can I help you, lady?"

The eyes came up and sized him out. She read the price tag on the clothing and saw him as just another hunk of big black man who couldn't afford her.

It was short and hard. "No thank you. There's nothing you can do for me."

Hump leaned toward her, savoring it and taking his time. "That wasn't the way you acted in there." His head tilting toward the game room.

Her eyes flew open then, showing the whites. "Oooooh...I thought you were Roy!" And before Hump knew what had happened to him, before she even knew what she intended to do, she drew the shoe back like a club and hit Hump on the head with the heavy heel. He didn't go down but it staggered him. And as he tried to reach for the shoe she hit him a few more times.

And then he started bleeding and he could feel the knot rising like a cake baking.

At 8:25, a young blond man, slim and two or three inches below six feet tall, sat on the small balcony of the townhouse at 18 Ardan's Wharf. To his left in the far distance he could see the blackish-silver that was the Cooper River. Straight ahead, but hidden from his sight, was the Carolina Yacht Club and High Battery. It was a mild November for Charleston, for being that close to the ocean.

In his movements, the way he carried himself and to some degree his face, there was more than a slight resemblance to the Alan Ladd of the early and late 1940's. In fact, from time to time, a stranger he'd meet while flying here and there or at a bar would note that remarkable likeness. At first he was pleased and he'd even spent some late hours watching Ladd's old movies on the T.V. Then around a year ago he'd read that Alan Ladd was so short that he'd had to stand on platforms to do his scenes and, one story went, Sophia Loren had to stand in a hole to kiss him in a scene. That was when he decided that he really didn't look at all like Ladd. Like a lot of short men he felt somehow cheated that he'd stopped growing before he reached six-two or six-three.

At 8:26 the closet phone rang. The man put his cup of coffee on the small wrought-iron table and moved quickly from the balcony into the bedroom. As he crossed the bedroom, passing the oversized bed, he paused just long enough to look at last night's girl, a sixteen-year-old runaway he'd picked up on a street corner in North Charleston. Her face in the morning light didn't show any of the night before. The slight pout to her mouth almost stopped him, stirring at him, but the dull, faraway sound of the phone drew him past the bed.

He unlocked the door with a key from a chain around his neck. The phone had been ringing about a minute when he lifted the receiver.

"Yes?"

The caller at the other end of the line gave his first name. He didn't ask to speak to anyone in particular and he didn't ask who the man who'd answered was. "Have you heard the news from Atlanta yet?"

"Not yet," the blond man said.

"A big thing happened here last night. Got a job for you. Five or six to deal with."

"The money?"

"High. A big pot put together. So much each head."

"Who?" the blond man asked.

"Don't know yet. Some soldiers are out looking. Read the morning paper … no, it might not be in there. Try the radio. You'll understand then."

"Nothing funny to this?"

"My word," the caller said. "How soon can you come?"

"This afternoon. Depends on the plane schedule, but by one or two. Two at the latest."

The caller gave him a phone number and the blond man wrote it down on a pad beside the phone.

"Done," the caller said and hung up.

He stood for a time looking down at the girl. He stretched, his eyes still on the girl, and the hard body of a dancer rippled under the robe. When his arms came down to his sides again he pulled at the loop in the belt and the robe fell apart. He dipped his shoulders and the robe fell on the floor.

Now that he knew that there was death in Atlanta waiting for him, he could feel the power surging in him. Even with the stop at Augusta or Columbia the flight wasn't more than an hour. There was time, plenty of time.

I had to wait until late in the afternoon to get the rest of the story from Hump. He'd been one of the last to be questioned by the police because he'd spent some time in the bathroom trying to stop the bleeding.

"Never heard so much poormouth in my life," he said. "Here was the biggest mess of big-time gamblers and bookies ever seen in one room…maybe in the whole history of America…and they kept saying, well, they weren't quite sure how much cash they were carrying, but it couldn't have been more than a hundred dollars. One after the other, the same shit." Hump laughed. "You heard me talk about Rance Carter, the guy from Cleveland? I just about choked when he said he never carried much cash. Maybe twenty dollars or so. That mostly he lost a lot of credit cards."

"He's the big roller?" I asked.

Hump nodded. "I never knew Rance to carry less than ten grand on him. Most of the time more than that."

"So, what was the take?"

"After the police add it up it might come to somewhere between ten and twenty thou," Hump said.

"The real take," I said.

"It might have been a quarter of a million and that doesn't count the jewelry and the furs."

"That's some evening's work."

"And my seven hundred," Hump said. "That's the ass-breaker."

CHAPTER THREE

Around five that afternoon I left Hump soaking and steaming in the tub. I spent part of an hour picking up a couple of six-packs of Beck's beer and a barrel of Kentucky Fried Chicken. As an afterthought I stopped by a 7-11 and got a big tube of Alka-Seltzer. If Hump was back in right shape it might be a long night. There was always the chance that we'd cruise a few bars so that Hump could tell his story a few times and blow in a few girls' ears to make up for what he thought he'd missed the night before. Not me, of course. I'd locked it up for Marcy since we'd straightened it out about a year before, just before Christmas. Not that the urge didn't touch me hard now and then.

As I turned the corner and headed for my house I saw a Buffalo Bill cab in my driveway. You could tell one of those without going to the trouble of reading the lettering on the side. It had the head and horns on the top. I'd always thought that was a little silly. When I got over the surprise I slowed down and tried to get a look at the driver or the passenger ... if there was a passenger. The engine was still running and the windows were fogged.

I parked on the street and got the sack of Beck's and the barrel of Kentucky Fried out and walked back down the road to my house. I cut across the god-awfully kept lawn where the blanket of leaves from last fall had killed off most of the grass. I put the sack of beer and the barrel on the front steps and turned and headed toward the cab. I was still a few steps away when the driver got out. He opened the rear door nearest to me and gave a little bow as a tiny little lady stepped out. It was hard to tell exactly how old she really was. There's a point after which old women don't so much seem to age as dry out and harden, until they're like those apple-head dolls they still make up in the mountains. Her hair was blue-gray and twisted into a kind of painful knot in the back. Above the hair rode one of those shiny black straw pillbox hats that you hardly see anymore unless you go fairly far into the country on a Sunday near the church hour.

"Jimmy? Young man, are you Jimmy Hardman?"

It's been a long time since anyone has called me Jimmy, unless you count a whore now and then who did that to pretend a friendship she didn't feel. And it was almost that far in the past since anybody had called me a young man. I'm forty, going on forty-one, and pudgy and neither seems to fit me.

"Are you or aren't you?" she insisted. It was the kind of tone and voice that a stern grandmother might use on a child. My grandmother had, and like any awed child I guess I was speechless. All I could do was nod.

"Surprised you, huh?"

I could almost swear that I heard her chuckle then.

The driver, a young black who needed a shave and didn't need the sunglasses, stepped in and held out his hand. "That's four dollars and ten cents. She said you'd pay."

I looked over at the little lady. She didn't seem anxious, just a bit impatient with me. "I'm not sure I know you, ma'am," I said.

"Of course you do, because I'm Annie Murton."

I shook my head. It didn't mean anything to me.

"I'm Tippy's sister." She paused to see the recognition-touch my face. "And I want to talk to you unless you intend to keep me out here in this cold yard all night."

I dug out a five and passed it to the driver. I took her arm and led her into the house and then went back out for the Beck's and the Kentucky Fried.

Tippy Farmer. I hadn't seen him in five years or so and I hadn't even thought about him since then. That last time he'd been in a booth in the Bluefish Bar out on Ponce de Leon and I hadn't known him then. But he'd known me. Maybe I hadn't recognized him because he'd lost the last of his teeth and seemed to be gumming his beer glass.

That hurt some, seeing him that way. I guess every boy has some kind of local sports hero when he's young and Tippy Farmer had been mine. It might be that time had made the image stronger, that it exaggerated it, but I'd been in a lot of major league cities and I'd seen most of the name pitchers, but I'd never seen one with an arm like Tippy's. I remembered those late afternoons in the summer (before the park had lights for night baseball) when he was playing for a local semi-pro team. That left arm that cut through the air like the whip of a length of rubber hose and the crack of the ball hitting the mitt, the crack of a limb breaking off a tree. But the failure was there, too. Tippy did two things well. He could rear back and throw as hard as anybody and he could drink as much white whiskey as any three men. In the end the white whiskey did him in. The Phillies brought him up for a try-out in 1940. He pitched two games in exhibition and it looked like he'd made it. But in the third game he started off wild and he'd been pulled, too soon he thought. So instead of taking a shower (he never was much on bathing) he sat on the bench in the dressing room and drank about a quart of good white whiskey while another pitcher finished the game. He got madder and madder and when the pitching coach came in after the game was over, Tippy cornered him in the shower room and beat the crap out of him. It took four men and a fungo bat to get Tippy off the coach. And that ended Tippy's major league days. Nobody wanted him and the blackball was out. He spent a few more years in semi-pro and then there was less baseball and more white whiskey. And then I saw him in the Bluefish that day. I started to slip him a few dollars, and I had a feeling he expected me to, but I couldn't. It seemed a little shameful. Instead I bought a large pitcher and had half a glass with him and got away as soon as I could.

❖ ❖ ❖

Annie Murton sat on the sofa with her knees properly together and her hands in her lap while I put the Beck's in the refrigerator and left the barrel on the kitchen table. Before I went back to her I looked in the bedroom. Hump was sleeping again.

I sat down in the chair across from Annie Murton. "What can I do for you? Is it something about Tippy?"

"Have you seen the afternoon paper?"

"Not yet."

Her purse was patent leather, old and cracking along the edge near the clasp. She opened it and took out a newspaper clipping. She smoothed it out before she passed it to me. It was an account of the robbery that followed the J.C. Cartway fight. I read it quickly, not really concentrating. I'd heard Hump's version and I probably knew more about it than the writer who'd done his dreamed-up reporting. But I took my time over it, pretending that it interested me more than it really did. Finally, when I thought I'd faked it long enough, I folded it and passed it back to Annie.

"I've heard about it," I said.

"No, the last paragraph, Jimmy."

I took the clipping back and read the last paragraph. It still didn't make any sense as far as Annie was concerned.

Detective Lt. Ernest Franklin said there were no definite leads at the moment, but he expected a break at any time. "At least I hope so," he said. "You see, there were a lot of mad people here last night and I've got a hunch if we don't find the people did this in the next day or two we might never find them alive. It's not a pretty thought but those are the facts ..."

I looked across at Annie. She seemed to be watching my face, as if trying to see if anything in the paragraph meant anything to me. I still didn't understand what she expected. I couldn't see what Annie or Tippy had to do with the robbery the night before. "I don't get this," I said.

"It's my grandson... you don't know him... I think he was one of the people who did this."

I guess I was too stunned to think. "Did what?"

"I think he robbed those people."

The blond young man, to the waitress who served him and the bar man who mixed his Scotch and water, looked like any of the hundreds of businessmen and conventioneers who came to the Polaris Room high above the Regency and rode the turning barroom while the Atlanta skyline seemed to move past. At the end of forty-five minutes, when the Room had turned almost its full circuit, he left a dollar tip and-left. He rode the special elevator down to the lobby and went out through the front entrance. The doorman, in his green uniform and odd-looking brown derby hat, waved to a waiting cab and he got inside. He gave the driver the name and address of a bar. The driver, looking at him in the rear-view mirror as he swung out into the afternoon traffic, sized him up as another visiting businessman who'd finished his business for the day and now was out to get laid. Sometimes, the driver thought, Atlanta seems like the pussy capital of the world.

The blond young man met the driver's eye in the mirror and looked away. He knew what the driver was thinking and he went along with it. On the long drive he asked a few questions about other bars and the driver gave him a card with his name and cab number, just in case the blond young man wanted to tour some other places.

Before the blond young man got out of the cab he , bent over and tugged at his socks, as if pulling them up, adjusting them at his knees. At the same time he adjusted the thin sheath on his left leg which held the knife.

It was time to begin.

I put the coffee water on while she sat at the kitchen table and started to tell me about it. Maybe I was wrong, but I felt she seemed much more comfortable at the table than she'd been in the living room. She watched as I spooned instant coffee into both cups and I saw a flicker that wasn't quite approval. I put the cups on the table and sat across from her, waiting for the water to boil.

"What makes you think so?" I asked.

I should have known better. I ended up with the whole story. It was like one of those Sunday afternoons when I was a kid, when we'd drive down to the country and visit Aunt or Uncle so and so. Everything would be fine until after the heavy meal. I'd be ready to go home and my mother and father weren't. The talk would start then, winding, circular, droning on and on and never seeming to go anywhere. Always seeming to be about to limp to some definite ending, but always gaining new life and spurting on.

That was how Annie Murton told her story. From the beginning, never in a straight line, important facts clustered together with the trivial. The beginning: her favorite daughter, Agnes, ran away at eighteen with the married man from the drugstore. She was gone for over a year and when she did return she was alone except for the boy and a dime-store wedding ring. She had a new married name, Robinson. She'd named the baby Edwin A. Robinson from a book on the library cart at the hospital. (Robinson was not the name of the man from the drugstore, Annie said; his name was Fergunson.) In a couple of years Annie and Agnes decided to move to Atlanta. It was their way of trying to protect the boy from the kinds of names he'd have to grow up with. Nobody in their hometown believed the ring or the story about the marriage.

Everything went well for the first five years or so. Agnes seemed to have a way with men but she worked hard and it was only on the weekends that Annie had to worry about her. But Annie understood that. Agnes was young and she needed a man just like a man needed women. It went along well until she met that Candyman, the one that Annie knew right away was a pimp. (And sure enough one night Agnes came home crying, crying so hard you knew her heart was broken and she said that Artie wanted her to do the same things with other men that she did with him. Annie tried to tell her there were other men, decent men, but she knew inside herself all the time that Agnes would go back to him.)

And sure enough, not one whole week later Annie came home from work and found the boy, Edwin, waiting for her. He said that Uncle Artie had come by for his mother and they were going out of town for the weekend but they would bring him back a nice present. It almost broke her heart, that small boy watching her to see how. she'd react, so she'd shown no reaction at all. She'd fixed his supper, fried pork chops and new potatoes and home-canned green beans cooked together and fried corn-bread and it wasn't until she'd put Edwin to bed that she went into Agnes's room and looked in the clothes closet. All she found there were the few rags that Agnes didn't wear anymore and the two white waitress uniforms. And it was like lead in her stom-ach because she knew at the age of fifty-five that she'd become a mother again. Lord knows she tried hard enough. She worked all day at the dress factory on Pryor and the boy was in school and she was too tired at night to do much more than cook the boy a good supper. ("Maybe that is why God made only young women fertile to the seed, instead of old women like me.")

The years that followed were good times and bad. And then when Edwin was sixteen he quit high school and got himself a job at the Burger Shack way out West Peachtree. Still, he was a good boy. Each week he gave Annie part of his pay for his keep and to help with the rent. But she never gave up trying to talk him into going back to school and finishing up. But he'd had the experience of having a few dollars in his pocket. ...

✤ ✤ ✤

"When did the real trouble start?" The story was true enough but I'd heard some like it before.

"Back in July when the state said that eighteen-year-olds could drink and go into bars," Annie said.

"Some people handle it and some don't," I said.

"Oh, it's not that. Any man worth his grits takes a drink now and then. No, it was the friends he must have met in those places."

I didn't like myself for it, but I was getting impatient. I didn't want to be rude to an old lady, my Southern upbringing made that a no-no, but I felt I'd heard enough of it and none of it added up to a robbery.

"Two weeks ago he came home with a shotgun and said he was thinking of doing some hunting," she said.

"Maybe he is."

"With most all of the barrels sawed off?"

"What?" That woke me up.

"He didn't want me to know about the shotgun but I found it in the closet when I was looking for some shirts to wash for him."

It was interesting but I hadn't bought it all. "What else, Annie?"

"He left last night without eating his supper, went right out the window in his bedroom. He was gone all night and the shotgun's gone too."

"Maybe it's a girl," I said.

"It wasn't a girl."

"Did he leave a note?"

"No, but I found this inside the screen door when I left for work this morning around seven o'clock." She unclasped the old purse again and brought out an envelope. It had some bulk to it, the shape about the length and width of money. It had her name on it in smeared pencil. It was money and I did a rough count of the twenties and tens and figured it at around fifteen hundred dollars. I put the money aside and looked into the envelope.

"No letter, no note?" I asked.

"Nothing but the money."

I put the money back into the envelope and put it on the table in front of her. She didn't touch it and her hands didn't even move toward it. It was a lot of money to her but it wasn't what she was interested in. "What do you want from me, Annie?"

She wasn't ready to say yet. "What that detective said in the paper, do you think that's true?"

"It could be. Whoever pulled that job got a lot of racket people mad at them. That can be rough and dangerous."

"Tippy said you could find him."

"Tippy's got a good imagination," I said.

"He said you wouldn't want to." She watched my face, intent, searching for something there.

"He's right. It's a needle in an acre of hay. If Edwin pulled this like you think, then he and the others in it with him have a lot of cash. Cash can buy a lot of cover. And the fact that he left you the money probably means that he's left town. That makes it hard. He's got the whole country to hide in. I wouldn't know where to start." I looked at the cup of coffee I'd handed her some time ago. She'd taken a polite sip and that was all. I got up and took it to the sink and poured it out. "Would you rather have a beer?"

"Beer's fine, Jimmy."

I got her a Beck's. "Best beer in the world," I told her.

"It's wasted on me then," Annie said. "I'm more used to Tudor or Red Fox."

❧   ❧   ❧

The fifteen hundred was expense money. That was as high as she could go unless she touched her burial money. But if she had to, if the money didn't last long enough, she'd spend the burial money. It didn't matter to her what happened after she died. The city could take her out to the dump and throw her on a trash pile for all she cared. "You see, Jimmy, Edwin might not be much. I'm not fooling myself about that, anymore than I fooled myself about his mother. But he's all I've got left."

I understood that and it touched me in a way that I didn't like to admit. To cover it I opened the Kentucky Fried and gave her a plate and a napkin. I left her to that and went in and awoke Hump.

"You're crazy," Hump said. "For fifteen hundred dollars you're going to put yourself in the middle? Right between the people who pulled the job and won't want to be found and the paid killers who'll think you're in the way? You had your head checked lately? Now, me, I wouldn't. ..." He stopped and looked at me with narrowing eyes. "Are you thinking what I'm thinking, Hardman?"

"You'd have got there sooner," I said, "except for that lump on your head."

"It's a foot race then," Hump said. "We try to get there first, save the kid if we can. That's the first objective. Then we get our hands on as much of that beautiful untaxpaid and untaxable bookie and gambler money as we can. Is that the way you figure it?"

I nodded. "As far as I know it doesn't belong to anyone. From what you said those dudes at the party didn't lose more than a hundred or so each and some credit cards."

"Count me in." He sat up and kicked the covers aside. "Where's that nice old lady?"

"In the kitchen eating your supper and drinking my Beck's."

Actually Annie had some of those old country manners. She'd eaten one drumstick and one breast and it took a lot of talking to convince her that I knew she hadn't come over just to eat my supper. With that done, it was everybody for himself and the kitchen table got lumpy with chicken bones.

Annie seemed to get along well with Hump. That might be because Hump had been at the party-robbery and that made him something special. Or maybe Annie had a better soul than most old Southern women do. While we ate and drank the Beck's, Hump questioned her about Edwin. He was trying for some feeling of Edwin's shape, how he walked, how he carried his shoulders, what kind of voice he had. When he'd satisfied himself, he turned to me. "There's a chance he might have been the one with the shotgun. No way of knowing for sure, but physically he sounds like he might be a fit."

"I was sure," Annie said, "but I was hoping I was wrong."

"The money nails it to the wall," I said. "How else does an eighteen-year old get that much money?"

After supper we gave Annie a lift home. Home for Annie was in southwest Atlanta in a neighborhood that had been working class white for a long time but now it was mainly black. Annie said she'd been living there for over fifteen years and she wasn't about to move. It was a square little house, like a child's alphabet block with a narrow screened porch and well-kept lawn.

We went inside. The house smelled like the warring struggle between boiled cabbage and Airwick. Annie showed Hump to Edwin's room and I stayed in the living room long enough to give Annie back five hundred dollars from the envelope. That would cover us for a week or so. If we hadn't found Edwin by then we might as well pack it up and give him a farewell wave. Of course, I didn't tell Annie all of that. She was upset enough as it was.

"If we don't find him in a week, then. . . ."

Annie didn't like my use of "if." I guess Tippy had built me up a little too large for real life. "But I thought. . . ."

"I can't make a guarantee, Annie. This is not like buying a set of pots and pans. But we've got a head start. Maybe even several days. We know or we're pretty sure that Edwin was in on it. That's something it's going to take the contract men days to find out. From what Hump said they covered themselves pretty well at the robbery. Now, if they've watched themselves as well the rest of the way, it's going to be a hard job for the contract people."

"What do you mean—*the rest of the way?*"

"Let's assume nobody got a look at any of them at the party. Let's also assume there weren't any prints left at the place on Rosewood Circle. That means the contract people don't have much to go on. They have to start somewhere else. They could start with the printing shop, the place where the invitations were made up, try to trace whoever put in the order. Or they can try to work back from whoever handed out the invitations at the Omni. Or they can try to work out who would know the house on Rosewood would be empty last night."

"I see," she said.

"We've got to hope that the rest of the robbery was planned as well as the job itself." I ticked it off on my fingers. "That the invitations were printed out of town or even out of state. That they found some way of hiring somebody to hand out the invitations without revealing their own identities or even get looks at them. That none of the people who pulled the job has any kind of traceable connection with the people who own the house or any of the houses around there."

That cheered her some. "And if they did?"

"Then Hump and I have some time."

I left her and went back to Edwin's room.

It was a neat room but still a slum. A single bed with a home-made patchwork quilt instead of a bedspread. A closet with a few pairs of summer pants and a couple of cheap jackets. A scarred night table beside the bed held a Radio Shack kit radio. Nothing on the walls. Hump had been through the chest of drawers and the closet. I sat on the edge of the bed and pulled out the single drawer of the night table. I dumped it on the bed and worked through it, putting it back in the drawer as I went. A pack of cherry-flavored little cigars. Several stubs from paychecks he'd received from the Burger Shack. After taxes and retirement he cleared $53.27. A copy of *Sports Illustrated* with the cover showing J.C. Cartway coming out of prison. I showed it to Hump and he nodded. That was another spoke in the wheel. A savings account book that showed, if he'd done his deductions, that he had $60 at First Georgia. A checkbook at the same bank that showed a balance of $24.56. A dirty book called *Blaze of Passion*. I thumbed through it. No pictures. That was about all, except for four books of matches. I scooped them up and started to drop them in the drawer. But I stopped. They were all from the same bar. Jake's Headhunter Lounge. On the back of each book there was a photo of a nude kneeling girl. And below the photo, *Topless Dancing*.

Hump came over and leaned past me to look at the match books. "It doesn't mean anything. Those matches are in about every hotel in town that handles the convention types."

"Maybe." I opened each book. In the third book there was a name written in ballpoint ink. Heddy, it looked like. I passed it to Hump and he nodded.

"It might be worth a try."

"You know Jake?" I asked.

"Don't think so," he said.

"We can try it. It's a flesh market, but Jake seems to keep his head above the shit."

"It's that or the Burger Shack."

"Both," I said, "but let's look at the titties first."

On the way out I laid down the ground rules for Annie. She wasn't to try to get in touch with me or in touch with the police. Hump and I would be covering some of the same ground as the contract men ... if there were contract men ... and we'd probably draw some attention sooner or later. Anybody who contacted us would draw some attention, too. I patted her shoulder and told her I'd rather she didn't have to talk with the contract people. They really weren't very nice people to know.

"But you'll call me?"

"Every day or so," I said. At the door I had one more thought. "And make sure Tippy keeps his mouth shut about Edwin. That could blow it."

She said she would. She'd dry him out or she'd put him on a bus and ship him off to visit family in the country.

Out on the street, standing beside the car, Hump lit a cigarette. "Something just occurred to me."

"What?

"If you were pulling a rip-off like this and you were recruiting, what would you use a kid like Edwin for?"

"For bagging the coats or maybe driving if his nerves were good enough," I said.

"And there he was being the shotgun man. That seem strange to you?"

"Somewhat," I said.

"My history's not too good. When was the Children's Crusade—1212 or somewhere around there?" He grinned at me and got into the driver's seat. "The more I think about the ones who pulled that thing, the more I'm sure they were all kids who'd just had their voices change on them."

"Might be."

We got on the expressway and headed for the Tenth Street exit. Then we hit West Peachtree and pointed for Jake's Headhunter Lounge.

CHAPTER FOUR

After we passed Pershing Point I told Hump to stop at the first pay phone he saw. I'd been thinking about making the call ever since we'd taken the job. It would give us an edge to know a couple of answers, but I'd been holding back. I wasn't quite sure how the call would be received. And, if the word got out I'd made the call, I might end up a fox rather than a hound.

Hump spotted an outside booth next to a service station. He pulled in. "That was a nice thing back there, leaving the five hundred with Annie."

"Not nice at all," I said with my hand on the door handle. "It's practical. If we have some bad luck, that boy Edwin is going to need a funeral."

The breath went out of Hump in a low, hardly audible whistle. "Hardman, you think too much."

He left it at that.

"Let me speak to The Man," I said.

"Nobody by that name here," said the man who'd answered my call.

"Then tell whoever is there Hardman wants to talk to him."

I knew The Man was there. Hump and I had worked for him once and we'd ended up saving his hide. I don't think he'd liked the way we did it, but that was almost a year ago and the last time I'd seen him he seemed to have buried most of the hard feelings. The Man's the black dude who runs most of the rackets in Atlanta and being in his bad book doesn't make running around dark streets in certain parts of town much of a pleasure.

There was almost a minute's wait and then I heard that precise voice I knew. "Yes, Mr. Hardman, what can I do for you this time?"

"How do you know I want you to do something for me?"

"I suppose you could call it a guess on my part," The Man said.

"I'll say this for you … you're close." I turned and looked out at Hump. It hadn't started yet but once we got in the chase I was going to feel shaky about being out in the open, unprotected. "I want to ask you a question and I'd like an answer and then I'd like you to forget that I asked the question or what your answer was."

"That is rather difficult," he said.

"At least it's honest. I could have tried to blow smoke up your nose."

"Ask your question," The Man said after what was probably a thoughtful pause.

"You heard about the rip-off party last night?"

"Yes," he said. "I understand there are some angry even right here in town or in planes headed for all points north, south, east, and west."

"How angry?" I asked.

"Furious. I understand some phone calls were made around town very early this morning. By eight o'clock a sizable kitty had been collected. Thousands on each head."

"You know who they're hiring?"

"If I knew I could not tell you. But he or they'll be the best. It's that kind of money." The Man paused. "There's one condition that goes with the employment. It is written in blood. When you find them, don't be neat, be messy, make it a message."

"Thanks."

"For what? You didn't call, did you?"

"Will he keep his word?" Hump asked as we crossed the parking lot and headed for Jake's.

"I think so. At least I hope so." I had the feeling that I'd both asked the question and answered it. And now that I had the answer, even one that I'd given, I could feel the load easing some. I liked The Man in a strange way. I admired his brass balls. But I didn't want some out-of-town murder squad using us as a stalking horse. The Man owed us and it was a debt that he knew money alone couldn't pay off, so I'd trust his silence.

"This guy Jake owe you too?" Hump asked.

"Yeah. If he remembers. If he doesn't I'll find a subtle way to remind him."

The debt went back a few years, to the time when I'd still been on the force. I didn't know Jake well then, but I'd liked the way he'd handled himself in a bad situation. There was a Mayor's race going on and the campaign people for the young challenger were going around to all the bar owners demanding, not asking, for campaign contributions. Jake hadn't kicked in. In fact, he'd thrown a pair of the more insistent ones out of his place. And then, sure enough, the challenger won and right after he moved into the Mayor's office the word came down: padlock the ones that didn't contribute. It was supposed to look like a new broom doing some sweeping. The day I heard about it the vice squad had already scheduled their raids. That night they were going to do their hard-assed thing. I went out to lunch and called Jake at home. I laid it out for him. He said he knew that it was coming sooner or later, but it was nice to have the warning. That after-noon, at opening time at his place, Jake paid off his girls and gave them a small bonus, sold his bar stock to a nearby club and put his own padlock on the door. He spent the next six months out in L.A. and Frisco and when he returned to Atlanta a lawyer who was working for him had squared it with City Hall. The fix was in and he could go back to running his bar and watching the girls peddle their hides.

After we ducked around a partition, we were in the narrow part of the bar, a kind of bottleneck with small tables and chairs in lines on both sides. Straight ahead the lounge widened and there was a small bar to the right and dead-on a raised platform some five feet above the floor. The girls had to climb a sort of a diving-board ladder to get there. There were more tables around the platform and to the right after the bar ended. Directly at the rear was a staircase going down to the restrooms and Jake's office.

It was still early. There weren't many of the business-suit breed sprinkled around and most of the ones I saw looked like they were college boys from Georgia Tech. I nudged Hump and we turned and sat at the bar. The lady bartender wasn't paying us any attention so we turned our stools and watched the girl on the platform. She was about six feet tall and slim, dusky, maybe with a bit of Indian in her. She was dancing that slow, by the numbers kind of shuffle that they all seemed to do, the dance they can do all night. The song was "Witchy Woman" and it seemed to be set at a level to drown out jet engines.

The lady bartender, with hair out of a wig shop and a face that was showing the night and morning hours, finally tore herself away from the stud at the end of the bar who was trying to get his tongue in her ear. I ordered two beers and gave her a five. When she came back with the beers my change was on one of those little trays, two ones and four quarters. When I reached for the ones she tilted the tray so I'd have trouble getting the change off it. I put out the other hand and tipped the tray so the change fell into my palm. She didn't like that two-handed game and for a second I thought she was going to spit at me.

"Tell Jake that Jim Hardman wants to see him."

"He's not here." She was mad. "He won't be in all night."

"You better tell him," I said.

Hump eased around and put his elbows on the bar. He looked at her in the way he might have watched one of those Navy V.D. movies. "You do it, lady."

It took her some time but finally she moved. As she did she ran one hand under the bar and hit the trouble buzzer. I knew what it was because I'd suggested to Jake once that he install it.

Jake came up the steps about three at a time. His eyes moved over the room, looking for the trouble. He was puzzled and a bit angry when he didn't find it. That was when he moved for the bar and saw me. His hand moved away from his hip where he carried a blackjack and he put the hand out to me.

"Jim, how the hell are you?"

"Fine. Just wanted to talk to you but I guess this lady works for you thought I was trouble."

The lady bartender scurried away. I introduced Hump and while they were doing their small talk I took a long look at Jake. He hadn't changed much in the last couple of years. Still lean and flat from handball and swimming, hair a little longer now that that was the style, a kind of brushy mustache he'd grown since I'd seen him last, the natural red streaked with gray.

Jake turned back to me. "This business? You want to go down to the office?"

I shook my head. "Just a favor I need from you. We can sit out here and watch the flesh."

"Fine with me." He crooked a finger at the bartender and she brought him down a Jack Daniels on the run. From the way he looked at her I knew the business of the trouble buzzer wasn't over for the night.

There were still a lot of empties around but he moved for one that was filled, a table at the head of the stairs where three other topless dancers were sitting. "Find another table," he said.

They obeyed like a trained dog act. One, a red-haired girl, in knee-length white boots, touched me a bit because she looked so damned young to be in the business. Jake saw the look I gave her and grinned at me. "Sit down quick," he said pointing at her chair, "and you can catch it while it's still warm."

I let that go by and made a point in sitting in another chair. "This favor has to do with a kid who might come in here."

"Lots of kids come in here," he said.

"Come on Jake," I said, "I'm not law and neither is Hump."

He nodded and relaxed his shoulders. "That's just reflex. Ask your question."

I gave him the name and the description of Edwin Robinson. At the end of it he just looked at me, not showing anything. "What's your interest, Jim?"

"His grandmother's a friend of a friend. She thinks he might be hanging out with bad company. I'm checking around on him."

"Jesus, Jim, I expected not to get the truth, but I thought you'd do better than a grandmother story."

"This one happens to be true."

Jake looked at Hump. "Word is you're honest, Evans. Is that mess true?"

Hump nodded. "Stranger and sadder than fiction."

The music stopped and the tall, dusky girl had finished her set. After she climbed down, the red-haired girl, the one I'd noticed before, slipped off a sweater and climbed up the ladder. It was a beautiful body, young and tight, with all the skin tone still there. For a moment, watching her and feeling my groin tighten I understood the kind of fantasy life that men who hang around topless bars must have.

"Like, you want to know if he's involved with one of my girls and might be about ready to hold up a 7-11 store?"

"Yes."

He jerked his thumb toward the red-haired girl. "How does she grab you?"

"Looks like she doesn't belong here," I said.

He roared with laughter and pounded his open palm against the table top. "You too! Hardman, I thought you'd been around the mountain and seen what was on the other side."

Hump shifted in his chair and leaned between us. I could tell from his face that he'd been taken, too. "What's on the other side of the mountain, Jake?" he asked in that deceptively soft voice that was three steps away from trouble.

"Almost nothing." Jake could sense it in Hump and I guess he decided that he'd better tell his story. "Hard facts. Would you believe that girl's got ankles under those boots that look like pincushions?"

"Is that true?" Hump leaned back.

"It's true," Jake said. "She's twenty and she's been needling for three years, ever since she hit the Strip around Tenth Street as a high-school runaway." He shook his head. "You want to make a guess what she makes a night in here from all the johns who come in and take one look at her and decide she doesn't belong here?"

"I'd rather not guess," I said.

"Most of the girls who wiggle their ass right make about fifty a night. Heddy makes a hundred a night and that's without late-dating and selling her ass."

"The kid was interested in her?" I'd tagged the name and it matched the one written in the match book cover.

"Sure. He'd come in and blow a week's pay in one night on her. If he'd been smart he'd have saved up three weeks' pay or so and come in on a wet cold night when the tourists stay home. He could have had all he wanted of it then. Let her fall under fifty one night and she'd head the whole bar for a fix."

"How do you remember the kid?"

"You mean why?" He slugged at his drink. "One night he blew all he had on her and wanted me to cash a check. Jesus, a check in a place like this?"

"You cash it?" Hump asked.

"No. Even if the check was good it was just money down the well." He finished the drink and sucked on one of the cubes. "In fact, I tried to give him some advice. I told him to give it up, to find a girl who works at the dime store. He listened me out but he was back the next night."

"He come in alone or with friends?"

"Alone mostly. I think I saw him one night with some other guys but I didn't pay any attention. After a time they all look alike." He spit the remains of the ice cube back in the glass. "That all, Jim?"

"I'd like to talk to the girl. The red-haired one."

"Heddy," he said. He stood up and waved a hand at both of us and went over to the dance platform. When he got there the girl, Heddy, stopped dancing and leaned over to listen to him. At the end of it her eyes flicked to our table. She nodded and went back to the shuffle.

A waitress brought us two more beers while we waited. I waited until she left. "How does all this grab you, Hump?"

"He's your friend."

"People change. Or maybe he's got his monthly."

"You wanted to see me?" she asked.

We'd been talking and hadn't even noticed that she'd left the platform. Now she stood behind a chair, still without putting on the sweater, as if she'd forgotten it. After a few seconds she pretended that she remembered and pulled the sweater down over her head. It was calculated, but I could see how it might work with the people with good intentions. Here's a little titty for you, she seemed to be saying, and you can still keep your good intentions as well.

"Sit down, Heddy. You want a drink?"

"Not right now, but you can pay the waitress for one and I'll drink it later."

"Why not?" I waved the waitress over and gave her a couple of dollars for the drink. From the way the waitress looked at me

I could see she had me tagged as another of those fish. I waited until she moved away. "Heddy, how well do you know Edwin Robinson?"

"Who?"

"The young kid who's been hanging around here. He seems taken with you."

"Oh, that one. Ed. He's a nice boy. Are you his father?"

Next to me, Hump put his head back and hooted. The hoot was loud enough to cut through the loud music. When it died to a chuckle, Heddy said, "I guess you aren't then."

"A friend of the family," I said.

"Well, it happens, you know. Fathers come in here to save their sons from me and end up with their hand on my thigh." Heddy looked over at Hump. "Your friend doesn't say much, does it?"

"Only when he has something to say."

Hump put his elbow on the table and planted his chin in the cup of the palm. He smiled at her. "Before we get social, Heddy, how well did you know the kid?"

"Just as a customer, a sucker."

"You take him home with you often?"

"He didn't have enough money," Heddy said. "He'll never have enough money."

"You meet any of his friends?"

Hump seemed to interest her a lot more than I ever could. I turned in my chair and waved at the waitress.

"He introduced me to a couple of guys one night. He acted like I was his high-school sweetheart."

I ordered two more beers and threw in two more dollars for another drink Heddy could have later.

"You remember their names?" Hump asked.

"I don't think so. You hear so many names around a place like this. One guy was heavyset, coal-black hair, about six feet tall. The other one was an inch or so shorter, reddish-blond hair, uneven teeth." Heddy shrugged her shoulders. "That's all I remember."

"It's a beginning." Hump gave her his lazy smile, the one that said all kinds of things to women, according to what the woman thought of herself. "They talk about any other bars they hung out at?"

"No. They might have but I didn't listen."

Hump looked over at me. That meant he'd run out of places to go and it was my turn.

"Did Edwin ever talk like he might come into some money soon? You know, like he'd have some money to spend on you?"

"Everybody talks like that." Heddy moved her eyes past us to include the whole room. "It's a big liar's game in here every night."

"Did he?"

"He might have." She looked up at the dance platform where the girl with the Indian blood was adding a body wiggle to the by-the-numbers shuffle. "My set comes up next."

I peeled off a five and dropped it on the table next to her right hand. "Where do you live? In case we need to get in touch with you?"

"Here."

"Where do you sleep," I said.

"Where I am when I get tired."

I looked at Hump. He gave me back about half a shake of his head. It didn't matter that much to him. He might have turned her on but she'd turned him off.

As the last of the Indian girl's record tailed away, Heddy got up from the table and peeled the sweater over her head. They were good breasts and the body looked like a hundred dollars a night. This was the private show for the five dollars and the two drinks, the money she'd collect from the waitress after we left. I was thinking more about the needle tracks on her ankles, if Jake was telling the truth, and wondering how long that body would hold together. Not long, I thought, and the dirty old man in me wanted some of her before it all wasted away. Wanted to taste the milk in her before it went sour.

I drew on the can of beer. "Had enough of this? How about a Burger Shack biggie?"

"All this stupid talk makes me hungry."

On our way out, passing the platform, Heddy squatted and did a bit of a farewell crotch-whip at us. Hump gave her the peace sign and we went outside, away from the smoke and the scent of all that green rank fantasy.

That was two more. Add them to the list. Find the first one and the others fell into place. That was the first law. But he didn't know their names. So he watched them as they passed the dance platform and passed within inches of the table where he sat. Get everything about them so he'd recognize them in the dark. The white one, forties, gone soft and slow, not a quick movement in him. Might have been different ten or fifteen years ago. Had lost it in the bars and the bedrooms and letting his birthdays sneak past him.

The other one, the big shine, he might think he was big and hard. He tried to cover it but there was a slight limp. The left knee it looked like. That meant he couldn't move that well either. And he hadn't seen or felt the knife yet. That would make him small. When it touched him.

When they were gone he sipped at an empty beer can for a few more minutes, letting the time run, waiting until the time felt right. Letting it build and grow.

He hadn't been in Atlanta eight hours yet and it was about time to cut off the head and watch the rest of the bodies twitch. Almost time. He ordered another beer by holding up his empty can.

❖ ❖ ❖

Hump was driving. About two blocks from Jake's I noticed that Hump was watching the rearview mirror. He moved over into the right hand turning lane and hit the turn signal. "I thought we'd go the long way." I shifted around and looked through the rear window. All I could see were the headlights. "I think we picked up a blue Impala outside Jake's. Might as well see if he wants to go the long way, too."

We weren't more than about six blocks from the Burger Shack but Hump made it a twelve-block tour of the back streets. The headlights stayed with us, close enough to see us if we got tricky, back far enough so it would be hard to trap him if we got on to him.

"After all this driving," I said, "I bet this guy would like a Biggie, too."

"If I remember right there's a package store up ahead. Got to give this side trip a good reason. Don't want to make that guy suspicious." About half a block more and he turned into the parking lot in front of Arnold's Package Store. "You need any booze?"

"Might as well." I went in and bought Hump a fifth of J&B and myself a fifth of Stock, an Italian brandy. So far we'd spent money that Annie Murton had given us to buy almost no information from a topless dancer and for two bottles of booze. At least you couldn't call the booze a waste of money.

I went back outside and got in the car and Hump got us going again. We hit Peachtree and did a right and in a block or so we were at the Burger Shack. Before we got out Hump cut his eyes toward the rear-view mirror. "He's still with us. If I remember the layout in most of these places there's a side entrance over by the john. We go in and have a Biggie and some coffee. You talk to the manager if you want to. About part way through I'm going to do my drunk black with a full bladder. You count ten minutes from then and you come out and walk straight over to the Impala. You see where it is?"

I did. The blue Impala had coasted in and parked several spaces down and behind us to the left.

"Maybe if we ask him right he'll tell us why he's stepping on our heels tonight."

We went inside and sat at the front counter with our backs to the parking lot. Whoever was in the Impala had a good view of us. That was the way we wanted it. I ordered us Biggies and coffee. When the pimply kid who waited on us brought the coffee I asked if the manager was around. That shook him some. Maybe people had been complaining about the service. He asked if something was wrong. I told him there wasn't, that I just wanted to ask about a boy who'd worked here until a couple of days before.

"Which one?" he asked.

"Edwin Robinson. You know him?"

"Sure. He worked this shift." But a thought had hit him and he tightened up. "You the police?"

"Friends of his grandmother."

"You sure?" He still wasn't convinced.

I held up three fingers. "Boy Scout honor."

That tickled him. "Weren't all cops Boy Scouts?"

"Probably." I gave him a grin and he moved down the counter to fill another order.

"What do you want to know about Ed?" he asked when he came back.

"You know his friends?"

"You mean the ones who worked here or the ones he had off the job?"

An idea hit me then. It was too simple and too easy, but I went along with it. "Anybody else quit about the same time Edwin did?"

He grinned. "How'd you guess that? Almost the whole shift." He nodded toward the grill where a balding flabby man was working up a sweat over fifty or so burger patties. "That's why Chambers is working his ass off back there. It takes time to train a grillman."

"How many quit? Five altogether?"

The kid looked puzzled. "Four off this shift and one off the shift right before this one. If you knew all the answers, why'd you ask me?"

"It was a guess." Next to me Hump was eating his Biggie and cocking one ear toward the talk. It was too easy. I could guess that he was thinking that along with me. But sometimes the luck went that way. It couldn't be called a mistake they'd made, because five kids quitting their job at a burger joint wouldn't cause much of a ripple in the world. It wasn't going to make the newspapers or filter down into the underworld pipeline. "I need a favor," I told the pimply boy. I got out a ten and creased it and put it on the counter. "I guess you've got some kind of list back in the office with the names and addresses of everybody who works here. It's worth this ten to me if you can make me up a list of the four who quit with Edwin … names and addresses."

He eyed the ten. "I guess I could do it."

"I might go out for a few minutes but I'll come back."

The kid nodded. "I get my break in ten minutes. I'll make you the list then."

"That's a deal."

The kid scooped up the ten and moved away.

"So easy it scares me," Hump said after the kid was out of eye range.

"Maybe not," I said. "We had a starting point, the kid, Edwin. Otherwise we'd still be chasing our tails."

Hump choked down the last of his Biggie and pushed the plate away. "Time to do my sneaky stuff." He staggered a little as he got up and had to brace himself a time or two on the counter as he moved out of sight. I marked the time on my watch. I'd been talking too much and my Biggie was cold but I ate it anyway. I washed it down with lukewarm coffee. I could feel the time ticking off. I waited the full ten minutes and then I paid the check and went outside. I went straight to the Impala. When I got close I thought it hadn't worked. I couldn't see anyone in the front seat. I opened the door and looked in the back seat. Hump was there and he had a necklock on the dude. I didn't get a good look at him. He had a screwed-up face and he was making sucking noises like trying to breathe.

"Like stealing pussy," Hump said. "Keys are still in. Drive us around the block."

I kicked the engine over and pulled out of the lot.

"This bag of crap doesn't know it yet but he's going to tell me everything he knows and when he runs out of things he knows, that's when he's going to start telling lies."

"The truth first," I said.

"Pick a dark street, something quiet and residential."

I traced, backwards, the way we'd come. After I passed Arnold's where I'd bought the booze, I saw a large apartment house ahead and to the right. I went just past it and parked under the shadow of a large oak. That blocked out the lights. I cut the engine and got out my lighter. I flipped it on and turned and looked at the dude Hump was holding. He looked to be in his early thirties, with a thin animal face that wasn't improved by a purplish birthmark that came up out of his collar and wrapped around his right cheek. He was still huffing and wheezing. I closed the lighter and it was dark in the car again.

"Why were you following us?"

"I wasn't . . ." He ended in a choked, muzzled grunt.

"We said the truth first," Hump said.

I kept my voice even and almost kindly. "Normally we'd take a lot of time with you, friend, and we'd let you lie to us and we'd lie to you and we'd still end up with what we wanted to know. We don't have that much time tonight. So I'm going to ask you one more time. Why?"

Hump must have relaxed the chokehold a bit. "You can go to. ..."

"All right," I said to Hump, "I believe in grown-up men making their own choices." I got out a cigarette and took my time lighting it. I took a couple of drags, giving him time to think. "Hump, break one of his arms. Make it his left arm. Break it somewhere between the elbow and the shoulder. That'll leave him an arm to eat with."

"I don't care whether the mother starves." Hump shifted his hold and now he had the guy's left arm out and away from his body. "It'd be easier to break it at the elbow, Jim."

"Do it the easy way then." I kept that even and understated.

Hump began putting pressure on the elbow. The guy stood it for a few seconds, about as long as I'd have taken the pain, and then gave it up.

"Stop it. Don't break it." It was a shade under a shriek.

"Who put you onto us?"

"Jake. Jake at the Headhunter Lounge."

"Why?"

"I don't know. He just wanted me to follow you around and see where you went and who you talked to. That's all."

"You work for Jake?"

"I'm the bouncer," the guy said.

Hump laughed. "That's job placement for you."

"You believe him, Hump?"

"I swear it's the truth."

"If you don't believe him," I said, "go on and break the arm."

"I'm not lying."

"Pass me his wallet."

Hump shifted him around and got the wallet from his hip pocket. He passed it to me and I took the driver's license out and returned it to him. Hump dropped it on the floor.

"What's your name?"

"Fred Maxwell," he said.

"Where you live?"

"Villa North Apartments, apartment 14."

"Where's that?"

"Briarcliff."

I started the car and drove back to the Burger Shack. There was an empty space next to Hump's car so I pulled in there and cut the engine. "All right, here's what you do friend. You go straight home. Get into bed and pull the covers over your head. No phone calls and especially not to Jake. We're going back to talk to him and if we have trouble finding him or if we get the idea he's expecting us we'll come looking for you. And we'll find you if it takes a month. And I'll let Hump break both your arms. You got me?"

"Yes."

"I'll do it too," Hump said.

"I won't call him," Maxwell said.

"And don't answer your phone in case he calls you," I said.

"I won't."

Hump pushed him away and we got out. I left Hump at his car and I went inside. The pimply kid saw me coming and met me at the counter. He handed me a tightly folded piece of paper. I thanked him and went back outside. The blue Impala was gone.

Hump headed for Jake's. I unfolded the paper and read the names and addresses. The kid had been nice enough to print them out in a child-like block printing.

Archie Winnson	*244 Tindall Place*
Burt Chandler	*244 Tindall Place*
Henry Harper	*112 Talmadge Road*
Ike Turner	*244 Tindall Place*

I folded the paper and put it away. It looked like at least three of the boys had shared a place. That made the hunting easier. Still, I had a feeling that we wouldn't find much when we checked the addresses out. If they'd played it smart they would have kept their jobs and blended into the woodwork. Now something had flushed them and if they'd decided to leave town it would be hard to find them.

Hump parked in the lot next to the Lounge and we went inside. The crowd was thicker now and the smoke and the smells worse than before. The businessmen were there in full force now and I guess the price of ass was getting discussed all over the place.

Heddy looked up from one of the tables and gave us a question look. Did we want her to join us? I shook my head and we moved through the noise and the people and down the staircase to the office. As soon as you hit the lower level you could find the bathroom by the smell.

I rapped on the office door. No answer. I tried it again.

"Maybe the guy crossed us and called him."

"Maybe." I knocked again. "Jake, it's Jim Hardman." Still no answer. I tried the door and found it unlocked. We went in and closed the door behind us. It was a junk kind of office. There was a desk and a chair straight ahead and a sofa over to the right where he auditioned his dancers. Once he'd offered to let me audition one but I'd passed it up. That was when I was first going with Marcy and it hadn't seemed my kind of action at the time.

The only light in the office came from a gooseneck lamp at the front corner of the desk and from the bathroom light that sliced across the room from the partly open door.

"Jake? You here?"

"Maybe he left for a while," Hump said.

I crossed to the bathroom and pulled the door open. He was in all right but he wasn't about to answer. He was kneeling, propped up, with his head in the toilet bowl. His hands were cuffed behind him and his throat was cut. Somebody had cut his throat and held him face down into the toilet and bled him like a pig. The water in the bowl looked as thick as pudding.

I left Hump staring down at Jake and went back into the office and called the police.

CHAPTER FIVE

When I got the police switchboard, on a hunch, I asked for Art Maloney. I hadn't seen him for a few weeks but as far as I knew he still had the night shift. After the way I'd left the force, resigning under fire, it was bad enough having to call and report a murder. All I needed beyond that was some kind of hard-assed cop who didn't like me handling the investigation.

Luck was with me. Art came on the line and I laid it out for him.

"That figures," Art said. "The robbery last night and now a killing. I keep meaning to see if there's a full moon or at least a moon that's filling."

I said I hadn't noticed either.

Art said he'd be down as fast as he could. "Keep everybody out of the office and don't let the word out. We'll want to talk to the girls and the customers."

"Right." Hump came out of the bathroom and looked at me, shaking his head.

"And keep your hands out of everything, Jim."

"He's got nothing I want," I said.

"A black and white will be there as soon as one can get there."

He rang off and I sent Hump out in the hall to watch the door for me. When he saw the cops coming he was to give the door a rap or two. After all, Art expected me to give the place a quick sweep and since he wouldn't believe that I hadn't, I figured I might as well go ahead. As soon as the door closed behind Hump, I cut on the overhead light and went to work on the desk.

Either Jake kept a messy desk or somebody had been there before me. There wasn't much worth looking at. All I learned about Jake was that he must have bought his Trojans by the gross. Well, he'd bought too big a shipment this time.

The two uniformed cops from the black and white came a minute or two after I'd given up on the desk and the room in general. I showed them the body and one of the cops, the young one, turned a little gray around the mouth. But he kept his supper down and I guess that was all you could ask of a young cop until he got his blood legs.

Art came rushing in a few minutes later. A police photographer was with him and a young plainclothes cop I didn't know. Art nodded at him and said his name was Bill Matthews. Matthews got my name and nodded at me with a look that said he'd eaten something for supper that hadn't agreed with him. Art took a look at the body and then sent Matthews and the two uniformed cops upstairs to close the place down for the night. More cops were on the way. He wanted all the names and addresses and he wanted the customers and the girls interviewed. Had they noticed anything strange the last hour or so? Anybody hanging around in front of the office, entering or leaving the office?

I'd given him the hour framework. Maybe one of the girls could edge it closer if they'd seen him after Hump and I had left for the Burger Shack.

Art spent only a few minutes in the bathroom and then he left it to the photographer. He came over to me and dipped into my shirt pocket for my cigarettes. His flat Irish face had a bit of a burn showing, like he was angry with me. "You find anything in the desk, Hardman?"

"I didn't look."

"Sure, sure," he said. He tipped his head in the direction of the bathroom where the flashbulbs were cracking. "I thought hog-killing time was December."

I didn't answer him.

"Isn't that right, Hump?" he insisted.

Hump gave him a lazy grin and flopped down on the sofa. "I wouldn't know. I'm a city boy myself."

Art took a couple of short puffs on the cigarette and then asked his hard question. "You two do some shady shit now and then, but you haven't taken up killing on contract, have you?"

"That's a hell of a question from somebody acts like a friend most of the time," I said.

His eyes stayed on me level and hard. "That's a message killing in there. You got any idea what the message is?"

I wasn't about to lay out everything I knew, but Art had been a friend for a time and I could point him in the right direction without involving what we knew about Edwin and the other boys. "This is just a guess." I told him about our visit, leaving Edwin out. And about the tail he'd put on us. "He was nervous for some reason. We came back to ask why. Too late, it seems."

"The why," Art said, impatient with me.

"Hump was at the robbery party last night," I said.

Art grinned at Hump. "Take you for much."

"Fifty dollars and a few credit cards," Hump said.

"I heard a story today. I can't say where I heard it. Some very big people got pissed last night. A kitty's made up. So much a head for the ones who pulled it. The contract's given and the work is supposed to be very messy." I jerked a thumb at the bathroom. "That might be the message. Nobody rips us off and gets away with it or something like that."

Art ran that through his mind for the better part of a minute. It interested him but he wasn't about to buy it whole without picking at it some. "Jake was a whore-master and a pimp and a few other things but I can't see him having that kind of balls."

"I doubt he was there. More than likely he had about twenty people who saw him at the bar all night. And he probably made a big thing of being out where he could be seen. But this kind of thing needs connections, somebody to plan it, somebody to get the equipment, the guns. All that. Maybe he slipped up some-where, didn't cover his tracks as well as he should. Or if the infor-mation money's good enough, some friend might have sold his ass, so much per pound."

Art shook his head. "I still can't buy it whole. The robbery was late last night. How do you get a contract man here so quick?"

"Local talent?"

"One I know here in town, but that's not his kind of work. If he'd done that there'd also be a pool of vomit in there. Couldn't stand that kind of butcher work. There's one in Jacksonville but I understand he got shaky and retired."

"Charleston," I said, dragging that up from some conversa-tion a few years before.

"Knife's his tool," Art said. "It might be. It takes less than an hour to get here from Charleston. I'll put in a call to the Charleston police as soon as I get back to the department."

"What do you know about this guy? I never heard of him." Hump was alert now, as if the other talk had put him to sleep but this had interested him.

"Almost nothing. Just rumors. As far as I know he's never been arrested, no pictures, no descriptions. No file on him at all."

The photographer came out of the bathroom. He dumped a handful of flashbulbs in the waste can. "I'm through here. Meat wagon's on the way."

Art nodded and waved him out of the door. After the door closed Art went on. "All we know is that somebody gets cut up and dead and the word on the street, a sort of whisper, is that the Charleston knife's passed through town. Been there and gone."

"I'll make you a bet," I said. "I've got a feeling whoever it was was sitting right up there, at the bar or at one of the tables. Probably there when Hump and I were talking to Jake. Waited until we left, got up like he was going to the john and nipped right into Jake's office."

Hump stretched and yawned. "Those girls work the tables pretty hard. Private dancing on the tables for a buck. Maybe one of them noticed one guy who didn't quite fit in."

"The bastard's too smart. He fitted in."

"You think it might be Charleston?" I asked.

"Him or somebody who works like him," Art said.

I nodded at Hump and he got up.

"You're not going to stay around?" Art said before we reached the door.

"We've got a couple of things to do. I'll call you in an hour or so."

He still wasn't done with us. "One part bothers me, Jim. What's your mix in this?"

"I don't have one," I said, "but I've got a nervous feeling."

"About what?"

"Let's assume that whoever it was is sitting up there, drinking a beer and waiting for his chance at Jake. Now he sees Hump and me come in and start talking to Jake. I wonder what he thinks about that? Has he put us down as being tied in with Jake? The thought of that makes me pretty damned close to scared."

"Watch your back," Art said.

"That and everybody around me," I said.

We reached the car and Hump looked in the back seat. "That was some joke you made back there with Art. That was a joke, wasn't it?"

"I wish it was," I said.

"So much for asking."

There was one question that neither of us bothered to ask. We knew the answer. Did we still have a lead on the contract people...Charleston or whoever it was? Not bloody likely. We had to assume that if the killer didn't know all the names when he went into Jake's office, that he damned well knew them when he came out. And there went the two or three day head start we'd planned on. So much for that kind of optimism.

We had trouble finding 244 Tindall Place. Hump had been sure he knew where it was but it turned out he didn't and we spent some important time trying to read street signs on dark corners. Finally Hump gave it up and found a pay phone. He called a dispatcher he knew at one of the cab companies. It turned out we'd gone past it a couple of times. It was one of those little two-block streets off Highland, mainly with those old wooden frame houses that had once been one-family dwellings when families had been larger some years back. Now they'd been cut up and partitioned into apartments.

We got our bearings from a lighted porch that had a big 230 over the door. Hump parked near that and we got out. I still felt a little shaky. I'd have felt a lot better if I'd been carrying iron or at least the slapjack. But at the time it hadn't seemed at all that way. Just a chase after a dumb-assed kid we didn't expect to find for a day or two.

"This is it," Hump said.

We crossed the yard. The porch light was out. I burned a finger trying to read the names on the mail boxes. At last I found the names and tapped the number. "Apartment 3."

Inside we crossed an old carpet, so old that you couldn't tell what the original color had been. The hallway had a smell of cooking grease and fish.

"Back there," Hump said.

There was a low-watt bulb in the hall and we could read the 3 on the door. I reached around Hump and tapped on the door. Hump put his ear to the door and listened. He stepped away and shook his head. I knocked again. Hump tried the door but it was locked.

"I can try to spring it," Hump said.

"It won't do you any good." I hadn't heard the door open behind us, but now I got the full force of the grease and fish stench. "They left. Moved out."

He was a little man, thin as a rail, with longish hair carefully combed back over his ears into a kind of ducktail. His teeth, probably false, looked as bright and regular as piano keys. I tagged his age at somewhere the other side of fifty.

"You the manager?"

"Oh, good heavens, no," he said. "Do I look like an apartment manager?" He preened himself a bit then, as if giving us the good side of his profile. "No, I just live here. I'm an actor, a professional actor."

"Sorry," I said. I reached in my wallet and got one of the Nationwide Insurance cards. I gave it to him and watched him back up some so that he could read it by the brighter light from inside his apartment. When he finished reading my con card, he held it by the edges, as if trying not to smear it.

"It's about the insurance on their car," I said.

"The van?"

I nodded. "It's some trouble about the rate. He didn't tell me the whole truth about his driving record."

"Been caught a few times, I guess."

"One D.U.I. on his records," I said. "When did they leave?"

"They left around ten this morning."

"Did they say where they were going? You see, until we get this rate thing straight they're not really insured."

"Just where the road took them. That's how Archie said it."

"That must be nice," Hump said. "Now if I could just work out a way of not having to make a living."

"Any chance of looking around the apartment?" I asked.

"There's no reason to," the old guy said. "They did leave."

"It's not that," I said. "A friend who drinks beer with me is looking for an apartment. Just separated from his wife." I gave him a smile and a tired movement of the shoulders. "It's been a wasted night so far. If I come up with an apartment he might like it won't be as much of a loss."

"I'm not the manager," he said. "I'm not supposed to open up apartments for people I don't know."

I got out the wad and peeled off a ten. "Call this a deposit on the key."

"Well, when you put it that way." He went into the apartment and came back with a tag with a 3 on it and three keys on the string. "Look around all you want but bring the keys back to me before you leave."

"A deal," I said.

The living room looked like a whirlwind had blown through it, lifting everything, stirring it up and then dumping it in the middle of the floor. The pile was up to my hips. I kicked around in it and decided that somebody's had a hell of a potlatch in the last day or two. There were balled and knotted-up trousers, shirts with the sleeves ripped off, parts from some busted-up kitchen chairs, pots and pans, newspapers, a few beaver magazines, pillows with the stuffing pulled out … all that and a lot more, all mixed together like a huge tossed salad of cast-offs.

"Traveling light," Hump said. He stepped away from the pile and sat down on the sofa.

"Not really," I said. "All that money and jewelry and those furs, that makes for traveling heavy."

"Next stop, new threads for everybody."

"Why not?" I said. "Looks like these weren't worth carrying with them."

Hump reached into the pile and brought up one of the beaver magazines. "And they outgrew these fur magazines and doing it all in their heads." He opened the magazine and leafed through it. "Which way'd you head? South toward all that Florida meat? North toward New York and all that variety? West toward the Bay or L.A."

"What's out West worth the trip?"

"Lord knows," Hump said. "All the women I used to know out there are all washing diapers in laundromats."

I stepped around the pile and went into the kitchen. Somebody had turned the kitchen table upside down and torn the legs off. I guess the legs were somewhere in the pile in the living room. "I wish I knew more about these kids. Where they're from? How much they've been around? What cities they've got their fantasies about? With some of that we might be able to come up with where they're headed."

"Big city," Hump said. "They could smell it, couldn't wait another minute for it. Had the best cover in the world and blew it."

"Or got flushed," I said.

Hump threw the magazine back on the pile. "No matter why they went or which way they went they've got better than a twelve-hour jump on us. Now you take New York. I'd hate to look for anybody in New York even if I knew for sure they were there. Not being sure and looking there, that's worthless crap."

No argument about that. Ditto every big city in the country. I left it unsaid and checked the rest of the kitchen. The sink was about a quarter full of broken dishes and glasses. They'd had a good time clearing out the cabinets. It wasn't neat but it saved a lot of time packing.

When I left the kitchen and started down the hall toward the bedrooms and the bath I got a whiff of smoke, old smoke. It was stronger in the bedroom on the right and I followed it there.

There was a metal trash can in the center of the rug. I lifted the can and uncovered a brown burnt core of rug underneath. It's a wonder they hadn't burned the house down. The can was empty but there was a fine white ash in the bottom seams. On a thought I put the can back and went into the bathroom. I was right. There was a blackish ring in the toilet up around the water level. That's where the ashes had gone.

They'd thought ahead. Maybe they knew somebody would be coming by. They'd burned everything in the house that might tell anybody the smallest thing about them. I checked that out by looking in the dresser drawers and the closets. Clean, not a scrap of paper, a letter, a bill or a phone number. All they'd left behind with their mark on it was the wreckage in the living room.

They'd put up a wall and called it a dead end.

From out in the hallway we watched the old actor do a scene for us. He had a worn old playbook in one hand and he was gesturing with the other and mouthing the words. But for all the mouthing there weren't any words except in his mind, so there wasn't any way of knowing whether he was doing Hamlet or Willy Loman. We watched him for a time and then looked beyond him at the room. One whole wall was covered with old photos and playbills, all tacked there in a sort of target design. Memories. I guess that's what you got down to in time. I just hoped it would be a long time before anybody stood out in my hall and watched me fast draw or do karate kicks.

When I thought we'd given him a fair hearing as an audience, I said, "Excuse me," and when he turned I tossed him the keys. He caught them after a chest bounce. Careful to keep his finger in his place in the playbook, he came over to the door.

"You interested in the apartment?"

"No," I said. "It looks like somebody took an axe to it."

His hand inched toward his pocket where the ten was. "Well...."

I shook my head. "Thanks."

We left him in the doorway, with the smell of fried fish blowing out past him. Out in the street the air was better. The wind was up and it felt like it might get down into the 30's by morning.

"Two things," Art said when I called him at the department. "The bad news first. It seems the Charleston knife's as much a rumor in Charleston as he is here. Oh, sure, they think he might exist but they don't know anything about him. No make on him at all."

"Give me the good news then," I said.

"Your idea about the girls checked out."

"Hump's idea," I said.

"Whichever. One of the girls remembered a man, probably in his mid-thirties. Slight. Two or three inches under six feet. Fair skin, fair hair. No facial scars. Nothing else that she took notice of. She said he was in the place maybe two hours. Drank six or eight beers. Sat alone at one of the tables near the platform. Let the girls cadge quarters off him but didn't want them to dance on his table for him, seemed distant. Oh, he was interested enough in the titty but he didn't make any bids. About fifteen or twenty minutes after you left the place … yes, she remembers you … not so much you as Hump … he ordered another beer and asked where the men's room was. She gave him the directions and the last she saw of him he was going down the stairs."

"She keep an eye out for him?"

"You know how things are over there. Some guy wanted her to dance on his table and then it was time to do a set on the platform and after that some other guy had a few words with her. The next time she thought about him might have been fifteen or twenty minutes later. She looked around for him and saw the table was empty. Went over to clear the table and found the beer can full, as far as she could tell untouched."

"Not much to go on," I said.

"The window in Jake's bathroom leads out to the alley. That means nobody had to see him after he ducked into Jake's office."

"He could be our boy."

"My thought, too." There was a pause. I could tell Art was working up to something. "Jim, this is the word from the mountain. I don't know your mix in this but if I were you I'd pack it in and call it a bad week. If I find you tiptoeing around me. ..."

I interrupted him and said I was out of it.

"Stay out then."

In my kitchen Hump had cracked his bottle of J&B and was having a shot. I got the top off my Italian brandy, the Stock, and took down a glass. While I sipped a shot I told Hump about the man in Jake's place. Hump heard me out and then capped his J&B and stood up.

"What's your hurry?"

"I thought I'd go home and melt down a couple of pre-war silver dollars." He was grinning so I wasn't sure whether he was putting me on or not.

"What for?"

"You ever hear about silver bullets?" Hump asked.

"Only one I knew used them was the Lone Ranger."

"Go on and laugh," he said, "but with that spook around, later on don't come to me and ask to borrow any of my silver bullets."

He was still grinning when I saw him out. I didn't know how to take him. I waited while he checked the back seat and saw him pull away before I closed the door and locked it. Before I went to bed I made a tour of the house, making sure all the windows were blocked down tight.

Maybe silver bullets weren't such a bad idea after all.

CHAPTER SIX

Marcy called around one a.m. and woke me up. I'd barely dropped off. "Do I hear naked women running around in your house, Jim?"

"Not women," I said. "Just one woman. You know I'm a one-woman man."

"Ha!" Then after twenty seconds of silence. "Ha!"

"Some long-distance conversation," I said.

It happened just about every time. We'd had a rough beginning and we'd worked that out. For the last eight or nine months I'd been thinking about marrying her. Even at my age, the rocky bad side of forty. I kept jumping from one side of the fence to the other. When she was in town I wasn't sure it would work. Only when she was gone did it seem like what I wanted most in my life. I guess I don't have the kind of optimism that it took to hire the minister and decide on the music I wanted the organist to play. But she'd been gone a week this time and the sad blues were on me.

"How much longer?" I asked.

"Three or four days. Four at the most." An aunt had died in Fort Myers and Marcy had gone down to help settle the estate. It was a small one and most of what she seemed to be doing was mediating. The old aunt had left a few good pieces of furniture, antiques, and all the relatives were in-fighting over them. If I knew Marcy she'd work it out so that everybody was satisfied and come home empty-handed. "What have you been up to, Jim?"

I gave her a short version of the rip-off party and the job Hump and I had taken for Annie Murton. I tried to make it sound routine, even the killing of Jake, but Marcy knew me and she had a good way of reading in the parts I left out.

"I'll give it another day or two," I said. "It looks like the boys have left town."

"Give the job up," Marcy said.

"We're just getting started on it." There was a high hard wind outside, the kind that pruned a lot of trees. The kind that made you glad you were inside, the kind that made you miss a good woman who belonged in your bed.

"Jim, I mean it. I don't make many demands on you, you know that."

I tried to keep it light. "Come on, Miss Badass, don't give me orders."

"I'll be back in Atlanta in three days."

Then the black silence that said, *say something.*

"I miss you, Marcy."

"You do, do you, you … you. …" She sputtered at me and the click sounded as the line went dead.

Sleeping in my too large bed. Hearing the windows shake from the wind. And thinking about her, also in a too large bed somewhere down in Fort Myers.

In the dining room below the Gilded Cage on West Peachtree near Baker the Charleston knife ate the two a.m. special. It was a strange group of people around him. All the waitresses, and waiters and maître d's and bartenders made a ritual of dropping by after the two a.m. closings for the steak and eggs. It reminded him of a meal he'd had once with a carny crowd.

The steak was a good cut and it was rare. The bubbling hot blood that ran down from the cut edge and diluted the scrambled eggs didn't bother him. Killing and eating were two separate things, not to be confused or overlapped.

But when the waitress leaned past him to refill his coffee cup he caught the salty underarm scent and that clawed at him. Killing and hard loving weren't that far apart. They seemed to feed on each other. One preparing him for the other.

The waitress moved away and he watched her go. Not her. Someone younger. But he'd have to be careful. Too much job left to do and he couldn't afford a mistake. He'd have to talk to George Beck and find out where the careful action was.

First thing in the morning.

"How'd the silver bullets come out." It was around eleven and I'd had several cups of coffee and read the sports page twice. Hump had answered on the second ring so that meant he was up and about.

"Wouldn't fit the iron you gave me. I think the barrel's crooked."

"Well, it was a good thought gone bad."

"Maybe they'll fit yours." Then a pause. "What's on for today?"

"I'd like for us to split up, cover twice as much ground." I held up the driver's license I'd taken from the bouncer who'd tailed us the night before. "The guy we persuaded last night. His name's Frederick Maxwell the Third."

"You mean there's more than one of him?"

"He said he lived at the Villa North apartments on Briarcliff. Talk to him and see if he was involved in the rip-off party. Might get something that might lead us to the boys."

"You leave all the pretty ones to me."

"He liked you better than he liked me," I said.

"And you'll be. . . ?"

"Looking into the other kid. Edwin lived with his grandma and three of them lived on Tindall Place." I opened the slip of paper with the names and addresses. "That leaves Henry Harper at 112 Talmadge Road."

"I'll meet you where?"

"Your place around two," I said.

"Watch your back."

"Ditto."

It was a neat house. Almost too neat. It'd probably been freshly painted back in the summer. And without looking you knew the gutters and the downspouts were spotless and the copper mail box polished to a bright glow.

The man raking leaves on the front lawn actually looked like he was whistling, he was enjoying himself so much. I put his age at about forty, the crewcut and the newly laundered fatigue jacket dating back to the Korean one.

It was the expression on his face that got me. I'd never been one for raking leaves. Nobody I knew liked it. The last time I'd seen Art Maloney with a rake in his hand he looked like he'd just started 60 days out at one of the prison farms. But this man looked like raking leaves was more fun than playing poker with the boys.

I went up the walk toward him, taking my wallet out as I went. I got out another of those Nationwide insurance cards. The supply was getting low. I'd have to get another batch printed. I supposed I'd been putting that off because I wasn't sure I wanted to pretend to be an insurance agent anymore. Sometimes it was all I could do to keep from selling a policy now and then. But so far, considering all the other possibilities, I hadn't come up with any other occupations that gave me the same kind of ready-made lies.

"I'm looking for Henry Harper." I held out the card and he stopped raking long enough to squint at the card.

"I'm Henry Harper."

I smiled at him and shook my head. "I must be looking for your son."

"What's he been up to now?" He put the rake down and without waiting for an answer opened a plastic leaf bag and began to bag his gathering so far.

"I'd rather talk to him."

"He's not here. He's out of town." He grunted. "On vacation."

"You got any idea where?"

"What's your business with him?"

"Just a minor thing." I kept it low and understated. "He was driving his friend's van and scraped a fender."

"God damn, he didn't say a word. ...."

"It's covered. No problem."

That relaxed him. "It was the Winnson boy's van?"

I nodded. "It's paperwork. Before we pay the claim I need to ask your son a couple of questions."

"The questions will have to wait a week or so."

"Maybe I could call him. He doesn't have to sign anything. Just answer the questions and we could do that by phone." I gave him my troubled grin and shake of the head. "The company with the lady's coverage is worrying the hell out of me. I'd like to get it cleared up, even if I have to do it by long distance."

He bought that and it opened him up. "He said the first stop was Jacksonville and then they were going to stop at some of the beaches on the East Coast. But he didn't say where they'd be staying."

I looked at the house. "Maybe he told his mother something he didn't tell you."

"My wife died three years ago."

"I'm sorry." To cover the awkwardness I gave the house another long look. "It's a nice house you've got here."

That rubbed his happy bone. "Isn't it though? Well, I keep it up the best I can. I mean, if you're going to spend all that money buying a house you shouldn't let it get run down, right?"

I tagged him then. He was one of those house lovers. Looking at him and listening I wondered if he'd loved his wife as much as the house while she'd been alive.

"Would you like me to show you around?"

I mumbled about other business and I'd take a rain check until the next time and headed for my car. By the time I pulled away from the curb he'd gone back to his raking, the brisk stroke, stroke, stroke following me for a block or so down the street.

I was through early and at loose ends. On the chance that Hump might be still at his interview and might need some help I cut across town and headed for Briarcliff. If I saw Hump's car I'd go in. If I didn't, I'd write it off as a drive to kill time before the two o'clock meeting with him.

The Villa North was a fair distance out and it was a smaller complex than its pretentious name had led me to believe. It was in a sort of "L" shape and I decided that they'd run out of money before they'd built the rest of it. Except that it had two floors it looked like vintage 1950 motel design.

I picked out Hump's car as soon as I turned into the parking lot. It was down at the far right end and I parked in a space next to it. I got out and stood on the walk and tried to figure out the numbering system. If Maxwell hadn't lied to me the night before, his apartment was number 14. Without too much effort I worked it out that the odd numbers were on the ground level and the evens were on the second floor.

I found apartment 13 and the breezeway and stairs that were between that one and apartment 15. My guess was that apartments 14 and 16 faced each other up there and I went up the stairs without seeing anybody. I reached the breezeway and found I'd been right. Apartments 14 and 16 did face each other and the name in the bracket on 14 was Frederick Maxwell, III.

I tapped on the door. No answer. "Hump, it's me, Jim."

Still no sound from inside. That bothered me. Hump had to be in there and if he wasn't answering there had to be a good reason. It didn't seem likely, but maybe Maxwell had got the jump on him somehow.

I tried the door and found it unlocked. I pushed it open and stepped inside. The room was completely dark, all the blinds and shades closed and no lights on. The only light was what I brought with me, the weak November sunlight from the breezeway behind me. I took it slow, one step and then another.

"Hump, you in here?" At that moment I must have cleared the door. I remember I was standing on a shaggy throw rug and looking straight ahead as I felt the whooos of air behind me as the door whipped shut behind me. I was in the dark then and there wasn't any time to think. It was all reaction, the body moving even before the mind had time to tell it what to do.

I swung my left hand out and gave a sort of karate kick. I didn't hit anything but I felt a sting, a burn on the soft bottom part of my hand. The same instant the throw rug scooted out from under me and I took a slide. The scared blood was pumping hard and I took a roll, turning and turning until I banged into something ... maybe the sofa and I knew that whoever was in the room would be coming after me now. He knew he'd put me on the floor and now it was just a matter of getting close enough.

I was trying to brace myself to get to my feet when I heard the soft *slep, slep,* the sound there for a second and then gone, covered up. He'd made a mistake and stepped from the carpet and hit the wooden floor. That was the sound I'd heard and now he'd corrected himself and I wouldn't hear him again. I gave up trying to get to my feet. If he was going to get close enough to hurt me then I'd let him have a leg. I waited beat after beat, knowing he was moving closer, wanting him close and then when I was sure he had to be only steps away, I made my only move. I coiled my body and kicked out with both feet. He was close and I had him. I wasn't sure where but the shock traveled up my legs to my hips and I heard the grunt that came out of him. It wasn't loud, as if he might have bitten his lip to hold it back. I said to myself, why the hell not? and I braced myself on my left hand and tried to push myself up. The hand seemed to be in a pool of warm liquid, slipping away from me, and I fell hard. I turned and tried to use my right hand and found that my legs wouldn't work. The shock, I guess.

The front door opened then and I turned to get my look at whoever it was and the light blinded me for a second and before I could adjust to it the door was pulled shut.

The sting and burn on my left hand was changing to pain. I got my right hand on the sofa and pulled myself up. The legs still didn't want to function but I forced them, walking stiffly, like I was on artificial legs. I headed for the door, where the light had been. I ran smack head-on into the door and I fumbled along the wall until I found the light switch.

My left hand was a mess. Not torn or chewed up but sliced through. The blood was pouring out and I got out a handkerchief and wrapped it over the wound and then used my right hand to clench the fingers on my left hand over the cloth. I hoped that would slow the bleeding. I got the door open and stumbled out onto the breezeway. I really wanted to sit down and cradle the hand but I had to keep going. If I'd hurt him enough maybe he was still in the area. If I couldn't catch him maybe I could get a look at him. I wanted my good hand on him but I'd settle for a look.

At the bottom of the stairs I ran into Hump who was on his way up. He did a double-take. He started to say something. I could see his mouth open but one of my legs took that moment to fold under me and I felt myself begin to tilt. Hump hadn't lost his reflexes. A big hand caught me and held me.

"A man," I said, "did you see a man come out of here … just now?"

"Sure," Hump said, "a dude with a bad limp."

"It wasn't Maxwell?"

"Naw, it wasn't."

"Where'd he go?"

"Drove off in a gray VW."

"Hump, you get a good look at him?"

"What the hell, Jim. . . ?"

"You get a look at his face?"

"He was turned away. Five-nine or so, blond hair. That was all I saw."

I held up my left hand. The blood had soaked through the handkerchief and was streaming. "I think that was the Charleston knife."

⚜ ⚜ ⚜

"In a VW?" I felt like a teenage girl about to giggle. "The Charleston knife can't afford better than a VW?"

"Take it easy," Hump said. He reached across me and punched the button on the glove compartment. He pulled out a large box of Kleenex and peeled out a big layer. He placed it over my hand. "Try to press the edges of the cut together. That might slow the bleeding some."

"How far to the hospital?" I was looking around but I couldn't recognize anything. I was lost. "We going to Grady?"

"Georgia Baptist. It's closer."

"In a goddamn VW," I said.

"Probably stolen." Then the thought hit him. "Why was he limping?"

"The same reason I am. I kicked the crap out of him and the only thing that ruins my pleasure is I don't know how good a lick I hit him."

The nurse at the desk in the emergency room wanted to know if my family doctor had referred me to the hospital. That was just the first question and I couldn't think of a proper answer, so I dropped the wad of Kleenex on the floor and started bleeding all around it. It made a pretty pattern like paint oh the tile floor.

Hump had an answer. He drew himself up until he looked about nine feet tall and he said, "Honey, you get one of those fat-assed doctors down here on the double before I start kicking the shit out of everybody in sight." He looked like he'd do it and the nurse decided to drop the questions for the time being.

The young intern, when he came, didn't seem to believe my story about falling on a coke bottle and cutting my hand. "It's too even," he kept saying.

By then I didn't care what he thought. Or what he believed.

Ten or twelve blocks away from the Villa North apartments the Charleston knife pulled into a Gulf station and told the attendant to put in two dollars worth of regular. He got out of the car with some difficulty and limped into the restroom. With the door locked behind him he lowered his trousers and looked at the bruise. The shape was clear and well-defined and he knew then what had hit him in the dark room. It had felt like a club but now he saw that it had been a heel of a shoe.

That pudgy son of a bitch still had some of it left. He wouldn't take him lightly the next time. And there would be a next time. Bet on it.

A few minutes later he parked the stolen VW on Courtland and walked over a couple of blocks and thumbed down a cab.

He was still limping.

⚜ ⚜ ⚜

It happened this way we figured out later. Charleston must have been waiting in the room for Maxwell. Hump had been there before me and he'd tried the door and found it locked. That was so that Maxwell, if he came, wouldn't think something was wrong. I guess Charleston could have opened the door and let Hump in, pretending he was Maxwell, but he probably wanted more of an edge than that. After Hump tried the door he left to look for the resident manager to make sure that Maxwell hadn't moved out.

As soon as Hump left, Charleston had unlocked the door. He'd set himself for the possibility that Hump would come back, maybe with the idea of forcing the door. Charleston must have decided that if Hump found the door unlocked he'd be sure Maxwell was in and he'd walk right in. Right up to the grip on Charleston's knife.

And I'd walked in instead.

"That's my cut you've got there," Hump said.

"You can have it back," I said. "I don't much care for it."

I called Art from my house while Hump poured us both a drink. Art sounded grumpy so I guessed he'd just gotten up after a long night over at the department.

"The Charleston stud is still alive and well and he's got a piece of my hide on his knife," I said.

Art was at my place within half an hour.

CHAPTER SEVEN

Art didn't stay long. Just long enough to hear my account and look at the fat bandage on my hand.

"Weren't you carrying?"

"You know I don't have a permit and with all those friends over on the force I've got a snowball's chance of getting one."

"The hell you don't have iron, though."

"I might," I said, "but I don't have any rounds for it. Burned them all on Eddie Spence."

"Remind me of that. Go ahead." But that cooled him some toward me and he decided to get a lick in on Hump. "And you, Hump, what do you mean you didn't get the tag numbers?"

"Next guy I see with a limp I'll take his numbers and send them right to you."

"Your friend's upstairs with a hunk cut off his hand and you just wave at the dude and let him drive away."

"Who said he was my friend?" Hump looked past Art toward me and winked. "Far as I know it was just two white asses cutting on each other. I thought I'd wait my time and cut the winner."

Art gave up. It was probably just as well. Hump talked him into a lift over to the Villa North so he could pick up my old Ford for me. He still had his back pretty far up when I closed the door on him.

Hump left around ten. He saw I really didn't need company that bad, just some pain-killer and some sleep. I got out my .38 P.P. and put it on the table near my right hand and watched TV.

After the news I watched an old Dick Powell movie where he was a private eye. The hand felt about as big as a balloon and it throbbed and Alka-Seltzer and aspirin didn't help. So I moved on to the calvados and I had a few shots of that and hoped that it would deaden the pain enough so I could drop off when I finally decided to try the bed.

Around one a.m. somebody rang the doorbell. I wasn't about to be taken that way. I turned the TV down and yelled "Just a second" and picked up the .38 and made a run through the kitchen and out the back door. It was in the mid-thirties and dark out there and I made it around the house in short time and lined up on the figure on my dark doorstep.

As I moved closer I saw that it was Heddy, the red-haired girl from Jake's Headhunter Lounge.

"You looking for me?" I lowered the .38 and held it against my leg out of sight.

Even without the gun showing I still scared her. She gasped and dropped her purse. When it hit the porch steps it sounded like she was carrying a junkyard in it. I made a mental note to take a look in there as soon as I had a chance.

"You always meet your friends this way?"

"You may be a lot of things, Heddy, but you're not a friend of mine. So we can cut the manure." I put the .38 in my pocket and dug out my house key. I got the door open and stepped aside. "You did come to see me for some reason, didn't you?" I said when she hesitated in the doorway.

Heddy shivered and went inside. I followed her and closed the door. In the heat of the house, moving behind her, her perfume had the smell of urine.

"So tell me," I said. We were at the kitchen and I'd poured each of us a couple of knuckles of the calvados.

"What happened to your hand?"

I'd seen her eyes widen at the mass of bandage while I poured the drinks.

"A dog bit me. Now, come on, let's not have all this small talk. It's late at night and I've got to go down for my rabies shot early in the morning."

She still wouldn't say anything. The hand that held the juice glass clenched white with the strain. I was glad I hadn't given her something thinner like a snifter.

"If I don't get my shot in the morning, I might start biting people."

"It's hard to talk about," she said.

"I might even start biting people tonight if I get bored."

"It's about Fred Maxwell. I think you know who he is."

"We met."

"He's disappeared."

"That might be the best thing for him right now," I said.

"No," she said, shaking the long red hair, "you don't understand."

"Tell me then and I will."

"I was just over at his apartment and there was a lot of blood all over the floor. Big drops and it was dried."

I sipped at the calvados and felt it burn all the way down. I decided it was better to let her believe that it was Maxwell's blood she'd seen. It might be the lever I needed. "And the blood was dry? You sure of that?"

"Yes, it was." She shuddered. "I touched... it."

"It sounds hopeless to me. It must have happened some time ago. Probably the same guy who did Jake." I reached across the table and pried her fingers from around the glass. The glass might not be thick enough after all and she might end up with a hand like mine. "What was Maxwell to you?"

"A friend."

"And what else?"

"He helped me... at times," Heddy said.

"He kept you in the stuff... right?"

She nodded. "Yes."

"You hurting now?"

"No, I've got … enough."

"All right then. Now how about some straight talk. Did Jake and Maxwell think they could rip off half the underworld and get away with it?"

"I don't know anything about that."

"Sure you do. Why do you think Jake's dead and Maxwell's missing? You need a few more bodies to convince you?"

"They didn't think … anybody would find out."

"Only one way they could have," I said. "Somebody sold them for bloodmeat."

"I don't know who did that."

"Sure you do. Where'd they get the guns?" I pushed at her hard. "Come on, you know."

"They didn't tell me. I swear they didn't."

I reached across the table and pulled her purse toward me. She made a late grab for it but I got it beyond her reach. I flipped the catch and dumped the contents on the table. Right in the center of it all was a little pearl-handled .32. "You scared of something, Heddy?"

"It's Fred's. I thought if I found him he might need it."

"So much for that thought." I scooped everything but the gun back into the purse and fumbled with the catch one-handed. I shoved the purse back to her. "Let me tell you something about a pro job like this. You never plan on using a gun. Iron's just for the threat, but if it goes bad and you have to use one you want to be damned sure that it's a clean gun. A gun that hasn't been used, new ones that disappeared during shipment or a sports store break-in. You want a gun nobody can trace to you. So if you're going to do it right you go to the man who furnishes them. He charges you an arm and a leg for them. Part of the price you pay covers his silence. As soon as he gets the money and you get the guns he goes blind and deaf and loses his memory." I took a slow sip of the calvados and let that work on her for a few seconds.

"I've got a feeling about this one. They tumbled to it too fast. I think the seller didn't keep his part of the bargain." I yawned and got up, stretching. "I guess Maxwell didn't mean much to you. Your supply, your fix man. Somebody you screwed now and then as a way of paying off a favor. Is that …?"

"They said his name was Middleton … Walt Middleton."

"That's better." I knew Middleton. He'd been around the edges of trouble for a long time. He ran a pawnshop down on Pryor. It was a cover for anything that he could do where he had better than a fifty-fifty chance of not getting caught. "Stay here." I went into the bedroom and called Art.

"What now, Hardman?"

"A bird told me that Walt Middleton furnished the guns for the rip-off party."

"Anything we can use in court?"

I thought about Heddy as a witness. It seemed hopeless. "I don't think so. The bird's too shaky. But I've got a feeling he probably sold out Jake. If so, maybe we can find out from him who bought."

"He'd laugh at us."

"Don't ask him. Just have some people go over and make him nervous. Hump and I'll pay a call on him."

"Right."

I poured myself a bit more of the calvados and I topped off her glass. "I called a cop friend. Your name's not in it anywhere. We'll see what we can do with Middleton. It might be the worst sale he ever made." I pushed her glass toward her. "Now I've got a confession to make. Hold onto yourself. That was my blood over at Maxwell's. As far as I know he's still alive."

Heddy shook the calvados all over me and the table top. She dropped the glass and put her head down on the table. She was crying and each sob sounded like a strip torn out of her lungs. I felt like shit and I wasn't sure why. People had been ripping her ass off for a long time. Why shouldn't I? Of course, there was no reason. But it took a bit of my humanity away from me and I needed all I could muster.

✤　✤　✤

When she was done crying, when the sobs turned to a whimper, I got her coat and brought it into the kitchen. She couldn't speak at first. All she could do was look at the coat and shake her head. I put the coat over the back of a chair and waited until she'd calmed down some.

"I can't go home," she said then. "That man, whoever he is, he might be looking for me. He might think I know where Fred is and I don't. He might kill me because I wouldn't ... couldn't tell him."

I went into the bedroom and got two sheets and a blanket and as an afterthought one of the pillows. I opened the sofa and did a sloppy job at one-handed bed-making. I went back into the kitchen.

"The sofa's made. Stay the night. Maybe it'll look better in the daylight." I handed her the .32 she'd brought with her. "You know how to use this?"

"No."

"In the morning I'll give you the two-dollar lesson."

I left her and went into the bedroom and undressed. In the bed, with the covers pulled up, I could hear her prowling around in the living room and the kitchen. Perhaps having another drink, perhaps a smoke, perhaps remaking the bed. And then, just about the time I fell off the edge I heard the creak of the old sofa springs as she settled into it.

Then over the dark edge, the hand forgotten in the burn and haze of the calvados, but trying to tell myself just before I fell, don't swing the hand out during the night, don't hit the bed frame. Until I didn't care anymore.

Awake. Not sure where I am. Confused in the darkness and in the dregs of the calvados. Maybe it was partly the wind rattling the windows in their old frames that made me think I was back in Japan that winter. Just before I killed my first man, an innocent Japanese barman, on a raid on a bar owned by some army men. In a bed a few streets over, behind the sliding paper doors, on a beanbag bed, waking with Kazuko hunched over me, tongue on my groin and moving.

Like that. Only it wasn't Kazuko. It was Heddy. Lost child's voice that seemed to come from a deep well: "I was afraid and I thought if I did this you wouldn't mind if I got in your bed."

Glad it hadn't gone past the point where I could stop her. I wanted her but not as part of a commercial transaction, not because she thought she only had one kind of coin to pay me with. Not that way. If it would happen it would be on some better day. "Forget it," I said. "There's no room rent."

Heddy moved up until her head was against my collarbone. "I saw how you looked at me that night in the Lounge. I thought you'd like it."

"Not the way you audition for a job at Jake's."

"It wasn't just that," she said.

"Go to sleep, Heddy."

Several times during the night I awoke and found her pressed against me, clutching at me in her dreams. All the brass and the crust that I'd seen at Jake's stripped away. But I didn't play with dreams: she'd grow it all back when she wasn't afraid anymore and the needle tracks wouldn't vanish so that I could run her for Cinderella. No, when it was all done, it would be the same.

And in the morning when I finally awoke to the gray morning sky, she was gone. All she left me was a burnt-bottom tablespoon where she'd cooked her morning pick-me-up.

Three hours later she was dead.

Art hunched over in his light fall topcoat. "You sure it's her?"

We were on the banks of the little trashed-up stream that runs through Orme Park. A little earlier an elderly lady had gone there to walk her dog. That was around noon. Crossing the little footbridge she'd looked down and seen Heddy's body.

Heddy was sprawled there, legs grotesque as a cotton doll's, head down in the shallow water. The moving water had washed the blood away from the cut on her throat. Now the wound almost looked natural, like gills on a fish.

"It's Heddy."

"Think her boyfriend, Maxwell, did it?"

I shook my head. It wasn't likely. Art knew that as well as I did. I guess he was just setting it up so I went along with it. "You could always use that as a reason for pushing a hunt. Wanted for questioning." I stepped back. I'd seen death a lot. Too many times. Maybe Heddy wasn't any great loss the way the world figures great losses. But maybe she deserved better than this. If death was obscene, then Charleston knew how to make it even more so, how to rip the last bit of dignity away.

A uniformed cop directed the meat wagon over the curb and down toward the stream. I didn't want to watch that so I went over and sat on the semi-circular concrete seat that ran around the water fountain. Art followed me. He shook out a couple of cigarettes and offered me one. He lit both and shook the match out in the wind.

"You weren't involved with her, were you, Jim?"

"Not with her. She wasn't my type, but goddammit, I think. ..."
I gave that up. An ex-cop talking about the value of human life?
But I had to give some reason Art would understand. "I guess I
feel guilty about some of it. I conned her and fucked her over to
get Walt Middleton's name out of her. That's nothing to be proud
of. I guess I could have taken the time to say I was sorry about it."

"Come on, Jim," Art said, "you sound like senility just hit
you a lick."

I just looked at him. He read me and backed away from it.

"All right, Jim, strike that."

I nodded.

"That pissed, huh?" He stepped away and yelled to one of
the other cops to stay around until it was closed out. When he
returned he said, "Even without an expense account I'm going to
buy you a drink."

We got into his unmarked car and made the circle and
headed back toward Monroe Drive. I looked back once and saw
the meat wagon grunting and snorting its way back over the curb
and onto Brookridge Drive.

Goodbye, Heddy, you with the beautiful breasts, the pin-
cushion legs, and the hot liquid mouth. In the next life come back
as a tree.

After the first drink I got up and dialed Annie Murton's number.
She answered on the fifth ring. She sounded a little out of breath,
like she'd had to run to reach the phone.

"Annie, this is Jim."

"Jim?"

"You know." I didn't like saying it but I did. "Jimmy
Hardman."

"Yes, Jimmy."

"Any word from Edwin yet?"

"No," she said.

"I think they left town." I told her about the murders of Jake and Heddy and that I thought they were tied in with the contract on the people who pulled the robbery.

"Then Edwin is in danger?"

"It looks that way. But if I can't trace them, neither can the contract man." That was just to make her feel better. With all that money working out there the underworld could put together a better network than the police or the feds had. It was a money pie and everybody wanted a slice of it. "You've got my number, Annie. If you get a letter or a phone call from him let me know. We need some hint to get our search going again."

"I will."

I went back to the bar and sat down next to Art. I wagged a finger at the bartender and he brought over the bottle of Bushmill's and poured two more shots. Irish was Art's drink and I could go along with that for two or three drinks. After the bartender took my money and moved away, Art curved his stool a quarter circle toward me.

"I've been trying to put all this together, Jim. I keep running head-on into one thing—you're not telling me the whole truth."

"Not all of it," I admitted.

"If you'd been straight with me, those two people might not be dead."

"Don't try to pull that con on me. When I went to Jake's that night it was for another reason. Didn't realize until I saw how he died that he must have been involved. And Heddy, if I'd turned her over to you, would you have made sure she got her fixes every day while you protected her? Not bloody likely and you know it." I sipped at the Irish. "Maybe I ran her away. I don't know. But if she'd stayed I think I'd have tried to find a way of protecting her. I don't think it would have worked. Scared as she was,

I think she'd have been out looking for Maxwell. That got her killed sooner than later, that's all."

"Without all the dressing, what do you know you haven't told me?"

"More than I'm going to tell you right now." He started to say something but I headed him off. "And don't tell me to stay out of this. I couldn't if I wanted to. That Charleston bastard wants to cut me and I'm pretty sure why."

"You're in his way," Art said.

"More than that. I think he saw Hump and me with Jake. That gave him the first thought. When I showed up at Maxwell's apartment that locked us into the rip-off party."

"And you weren't?"

"Sure I was. And I sent Hump to the party so he could get his roll taken and get his head beaten in."

"All right, all right." He put his head back and threw down the last half shot of Irish. "But you're going to have to talk to me before the week's out. I can't swim in this sewer blind." He got up and struggled into his topcoat. "You want me to drop you somewhere?"

"I'll get Hump to pick me up." I stopped him before he started for the door. "Is the pressure on Middleton?"

Art checked his watch. "It's been going on the last hour or so. A squad's down there taking the place apart brick by brick. All I hope is that we find one thing that's been stolen, just one. Something to pry at him with. But he's too slick. The shop'll be clean."

"When's the hunt over?"

"Maybe another hour."

"Hump and I'll drop in on Walt after that."

"Nothing rough," Art said.

"Nothing he'll tell the cops about."

Art nodded. "Better that way."

Hump came over about forty-five minutes later. We had a couple of beers and waited out the time margin that Art had given us. We wanted the cops gone for a time before we showed. I didn't want Walt to make any kind of connection between the squad's business and our visit. I just wanted it to look like one of those bad days when the roof falls in.

"How do we work it?" Hump wanted to know.

"Whipsaw," I said. I held up the bandaged left hand. "This got me my part."

"Someday," Hump sighed, "just someday I want the pissed-off part. Reasonable crap tires me."

CHAPTER EIGHT

W alt had thickened some around the waist since I'd last seen him, since I'd tried to bust him over some jewelry I was sure he'd contracted to fence. That had been about four years ago. It hadn't worked then but I'd had a good look inside him. His eyes as he recognized me, as they darted from me to Hump and back, made me sure that I'd read him right. We could break his bones and pour the marrow out.

"Mr. Hardman, isn't it? It's been a long time since I've seen you."

"Four years."

"I hear you're not with the police anymore." He was talking to me but he was watching Hump who'd drifted away, back toward the rear of the pawnshop. Hump did it so you could read it from a mile away: he was checking the place for other customers and for any employees Walt might have working back there.

"I gave it up for my health," I said.

Walt gave a kind of jerky ha-ha. "That's not what I heard, but I'm not judging."

"I hope not."

Hump returned as casually as he'd moved away. He stared at Walt for a second and then nodded at me.

Walt saw that. He was supposed to. It shook him and the first crack appeared in his backbone. "What can I do for you and your friend, Mr. Hardman?"

"You could tell me a few things," I said.

"Anything I can," Walt said expansively. "You know I respected you when you were with the police."

"That makes it a lot easier then." I held up the bandaged hand. "Somebody tried to stick a blade in my liver."

"Terrible what these young punks will do," Walt said. "It must have been some junk-user trying for your roll."

"That's a good plot, Walt. I think you ought to make a short story out of it." I turned to Hump. "What's the dude's name anyway?"

"Charleston," Hump said. "Some people call him the Charleston knife."

"I've never heard of him," Walt said. "Is he a local man?"

I didn't show anything at the lie. I gave Hump a sad, slow shake of my head. "I told you on the way over here that Walt wouldn't lie to me, didn't I? That he might lie to some people, but not to me."

"That's what you said." Hump sounded bored with it all. "A man lies when he's hiding something."

"Why should I lie?" Walt wrapped the sincere indignation around him. "I keep an honest pawnshop and I pay my taxes and...."

"And love your mother ... and lie to people," I said.

"Mr. Hardman, with God as my witness, I wouldn't lie to you."

"Let's hope God's busy somewhere and not listening," Hump said. "False swearing can get you in trouble."

The crack in the bone widened. "I swear...."

"See? You keep doing that." Hump gave him an insolent grin.

My turn. "I got it on a good source, Walt, that you furnished the clean iron for the robbery a couple of nights ago."

"That's a lie," Walt shrieked. "A fucking lie."

"You calling me a liar, Walt?" I looked over at Hump. "What you think about this tub of guts calling me a liar?"

"Easy, Jim. That'll make trouble."

Hump's reasonable tone was a good one to play against. "I don't give a shit. I've already got trouble. Look at this turd. He sells the clean iron, takes their money, and then he turns right around and sells them out. Makes bloodmeat out of them." I waved the hand around and it began to ache. "And I almost end up buying the farm because I know one of them. No, you're not going to lie to me, Walt, because I'll kick your ass from here to Decatur before I let you."

Hump moved over and got a grip on my good hand. "Come on. How'd he know he was getting you in the line of fire? Be smart, Jim. How could he know?"

Walt wasn't sure quite how to play this. Nodding seemed to be easier because Hump was holding me back, but nodding meant that he'd be admitting something he didn't want to. On the other hand, denying it might make me break bad and come over the counter after him. Back when I'd known him I'd had a hard reputation and I guess he remembered it. With that choice before him he decided to nod. It was a tentative nod, one so brief that perhaps he hoped we'd miss it. We didn't.

"What you say, Walt?" Hump pushed at him.

It came out choked. "I didn't know. I swear it."

"You see, Jim? It's not his fault. That's what I've been trying to tell you all day. Hell, he'd probably walk around the block rather than get you in trouble. Right, Walt?"

"Sure. If I'd known they'd come after you, I'd have thought about it twice."

"Calm down, Jim," Hump said. "Walt'll find some way to square it with you."

"I'll do anything I can." But Walt was beginning to get his second wind and the bone would have to break the rest of the way quick or he'd find a way to lie out of it.

"Wake up, Hump. He's going to cheap shit con us. Look at him. Right now he thinks he's out of the woods and he's running a few lies past just to decide which one he'll use on us. And after we leave he'll be laughing up his armpit at us."

"He better not be," Hump said. He released my arm and stepped away.

I moved to the counter and let him smell the Irish and the beer fumes. "You sold out Jake and the rest of the bunch. So far Jake and a girl who worked for him are dead. Butchered, bled like hogs. Now that's your fault and you've got twenty-five words or so to convince me there's some reason why you ought to be living."

"I couldn't help It," Walt said.

I turned to Hump. "Count the words. That's four he's wasted so far." I swung back at Walt. "Charleston's got his wires crossed. He's trying to cut me. You better pick your side and you better pick the winner. If he wins you're free and clear. If he loses and you haven't been straight with me you'll end up in dog food cans."

"If it helps you make your choice," Hump said, "I'm with Hardman and the dude who's going to cut me is still in his daddy's gonads."

"What do you want to know?"

"Six more words," I said to Hump. "That makes ten." Back to Walt: "I want to know who you sold them out to."

"I can't. ..." Walt stopped himself. He realized that the protest just ran the word count up.

"Make your bet," I said.

"And I never talked to you?"

"I haven't seen you in years. I don't even know you."

The bone broke the rest of the way. "A soldier named Bert Wolff came by the morning after. He was checking the dealers, all the ones who furnish guns for jobs. He roughed me up and I told him. They didn't pay me anything. They didn't even offer me anything. But they said they'd kill me if I didn't tell."

I vaguely remembered the soldier's name. "Who does Bert soldier for?"

"I heard it was Jocko."

"Just heard?" I said.

"No, he told me Jocko sent him."

That would be Eddie Giacommo. He owned an Italian restaurant and owned pieces of some bars and topless places. The restaurant, The Gondola, was considered the best Italian eating place in town. I'd eaten there a few times. The last time I'd taken Marcy there Eddie had made a big thing over admiring her. And he'd sent a bottle of his private stock over to the table. So much for that kind of old-country courtesy. If Jocko was running the hunt, a nodding acquaintance with me wouldn't buy me much. In that hunt business nobody knows the names of the foxes.

"We'll cover you," I told Walt.

"The way you covered Jake and the others?" Walt didn't seem that sure.

"Better," I said, "a lot better."

"Jocko? I thought he was out of that kind of thing." Art was talking in a whisper. That meant there was company around. "His name hasn't bounced around the shop for months."

"See if Intelligence has an up-date."

"And meet you where?"

"The Coffee Shop."

"It'll be an hour. Still got paperwork on the girl."

"Soon as you can," I said. "Dark's around six and I don't feel comfortable out with that cutter around."

"Forty-five minutes," Art said.

Hump took his time driving over to The Coffee Shop. It wasn't much to rush across town for. The cooking was said to be like mother's but to Southerners that meant overcooked and greasy with ham fat. It'd been a bad night and a hard day and I could feel a headache coming on. No lunch and those drinks with Art and then those beers. Maybe I'd have felt better with something to eat, but after seeing Heddy in that stream-ditch I wasn't sure I'd eat for another week.

"You look dragging," Hump said.

"A snake's belly," I said.

"The girl?"

I was watching the street. It was cold and gray, the kind of day to be in bed with a woman you loved if you had one. If not, then one you liked and could talk to. Marcy. I guess she was one or both of those.

It wasn't a good day to be found face down in the water.

"It's not all that Mike Hammer shit. A mixture of the sad blues and pissed off." Human life ought to mean more than that. Jocko birddogs and does his point and Charleston rushes right over and cuts a throat. And all the time Jocko's sitting in the back booth in the front room of The Gondola drinking coffee and looking for all the world like the kindly old country host. If anything bothered him it didn't show while he lunched on veal or moved through the lunch crowd, bestowing his recognition upon a choice table or two. Nothing showing on him. Money and pride washing over him while the bones and bloodmeat got made somewhere else.

I decided it would be better not to say much of that. "You ever meet Jocko, Hump?"

"Me? I'm a spaghetti and meatballs man. You reckon they serve that over at his place?"

"Probably."

"I met him once. A year ago. You know Harve White, locates and runs a game now and then? Takes a percentage out of each pot. Skinny little guy always got a cough?"

"I know him," I said.

"I was short one time. Some girl screwed me to sleep and ran off with my roll. So Harve comes up and asks if I'd be doorman for him. You might remember about that time some guys were knocking over games?"

I remembered. It seemed to be a sport that caught on now and then. No income tax and nothing on your police bands because the robberies never got reported. But sooner or later a couple of the studs would be burned bad and the sport would wash away.

Hump parked in the lot across from The Coffee Shop. Neither of us made a move to get out. There was still a lot of time before we expected Art.

"I'm good for a touch," I said. "You could have come to me."

"And admit some dog rolled me? I feel funny telling about it now. Anyway Harve offered me a hundred the night. I'd meet them at the door, check their names against the list. Nobody in who wasn't on the list. And no iron in the room. Iron to be checked with me out in the hall. No trouble the first hour or so. They're drifting in one or two at the time. Going to the bar Harve's set up. No trouble until those two show up. Jocko and his shadow. Jocko's all sleek and pampered. Dark suit with a white silk tie. Handmade shoes. Sweet and kindly. Not the shadow with him. He's all rock and rough edges. No make-believe about him, no smokestacking about him. He's the real article. Now I see the bulge and I know he's carrying and he tries to waltz right past me. The last thing I want to do is mess with him but when you take a man's money you take the rank with it. So sweet as a tea party I tell him there's no iron in the game room and he's got to check it with me. For a second it's tight. Hardrock didn't want to give it up. He says nobody touches his iron and I go over to this dresser where I've put the guns and I pull out a drawer and I say he can put it in himself and take it out himself after the game's over. He still doesn't like it but Jocko's been looking at me like I'm one of his black dishwashers or busboys and he tells Hardrock to go ahead and leave the iron. Then he grins at me and says something like he's sure Hardrock won't have any trouble making me give it back."

"Would he have had trouble?"

"I'm not sure. He's one hardcocked dude and he might have been more than I could handle."

"You might meet him again if he's still working for Jocko."

"I'm running that around in my head, have been since Walt gave us the name. Might have to head-on with him."

"It comes to that I'll help you," I said, grinning.

"You?" The laugh was friendly but there was some truth in it. "A fat nice dude like you with one good hand?"

"Come on, now, don't hurt my feelings."

"Wouldn't do that." Hump opened his ash tray and took out a short, half-smoked joint. He lit it and did that hissing and smoked it off. He didn't offer me any but it wasn't unfriendly. At first he had and now I guess he'd decided to save his breath. When he was done, he stubbed it out and we went across the street to wait for Art.

"The recent file's flat as my bankbook," Art said. "I made the trip so you could buy me supper."

"Order," I said.

I passed up a menu and Hump looked a question at me. I shook my head. "We might try the spaghetti and meatballs later."

Art ordered and Hump and I took another beer. Art watched the waitress out of earshot. "Almost nothing on Jocko in the last year. If he's doing anything he's hiding it well. Maybe four or five trips to New York this year so far. No way of knowing what his business was up there. Two trips to Miami. Same blank there."

"Strange traffic around him since the robbery?"

"Nobody new that we know."

"Why's Jocko running the hunt?" I asked.

"Maybe pride. This is his preserve, his playground and he runs a tight ship. Looks bad when somebody gets out of hand and rips off half the big-time game people. Looks like he can't keep the rabble in line. More than that he's making points for himself, collecting I.O.U.'s he can call later if he needs a favor."

"Any calls to Charleston since Monday?"

"You know better than that. He's going to use his office or home phone for that? Not while all you need is a handful of quarters and a pay phone."

Hump tilted his head back and poured his beer down. "Who's his shadow now? The same one from a year or so ago?"

Art nodded. "If we're thinking about the same one. Not quite as wide as a door but he looks like he knows how to make you hurt. Some old acne scars across his nose and high on his cheekbones?"

"That's him," Hump said.

"His name's George Beck. And I'll tell you this story about him. It got hushed up at the time. A fall ago three tough guys from one of the pro teams...I don't remember whether it was the 49-ers or the Bears...went into The Gondola. Had too much to drink and decided to terrorize the place. Jocko just nodded at George and turned him loose. He cleaned plows and handles and harness and he had those boys out on the street before they knew what hit them."

"What did hit them?" Hump asked.

"Mostly fists. Maybe a high kick or two. Word is he might have been a pug one time." Art hadn't read much into the questions at first. Now it hit him that there was more than a casual interest at work here. "You know him, Hump?"

"Met him once."

"Bad blood?"

"Some," Hump said.

"You're not thinking of going against him, are you?"

"Of course not." Hump grinned at Art. "You think I got crap for brains?"

"If you decided to I'll take an invitation. I'd like to see it."

"No," Hump said, "you wouldn't want to see it."

Art's supper came and I gave the waitress some money to cover his meal, our beers, and a tip. We got in Hump's car and sat there. He didn't make a move to turn the engine over. Just sat there moving his shoulders as if trying to get a chill out of him. Then he lit a cigarette and looked at me. "I'm getting so I can read your foxy mind, Hardman, and right now you're trying to think up a way you can give me an out, let me slide away from it."

"That's close," I said.

"What's hard is that you've got to find a way that'll leave me some balls."

"Closer and closer," I said.

"Of course, nothing might come of it. We might just end up eating the spaghetti and meatballs."

"And drinking the wine."

"And drinking the wine," Hump said. He kicked the engine over and grinned at me. "Appreciate you worrying about me. And if it makes you worry less there is some badass in me you've never seen." He made his circle and pulled out of the parking lot.

"We'll leave it at that and float with it."

"Agreed."

God, Beck said, you ought to be in the movies, the ones they show on Houston Street.

I have a good day now and then, the blond young man said.

I'd take one of your bad days, Beck said.

It's all in the mind, the blond man said.

Beck was driving. Where now? he asked.

The blond man gave him an address. He'd checked it on an Atlanta street map and his directions were precise.

More girls? Beck asked.

Boys, the blond man said.

The maître d' wanted to seat us in the inner room, the one where the bandstand was, where the eunuch-looking Danish tenor sang Italian songs. I'd made that mistake once and almost lost the hearing in one ear. Also I'd almost eaten a napkin by mistake because the lighting was low and romantic in there.

Last of all, Jocko was at his usual booth and it might be a way of getting it started. Sitting under his nose and seeing what came of it. I knew Jocko had seen us enter but he pretended that he hadn't. Head down over his account books. Let him play act all he wanted to.

I held out against the maître d' and ended up with a table almost directly across from Jocko. The shadow, George Beck, wasn't around.

The waiter came and I ordered the antipasto and the scampi. Hump nodded along with the antipasto and got his inner laugh by ordering the spaghetti and meatballs. As soon as we'd finished ordering, almost as if on a signal, Jocko looked up and gave me a surprised look of recognition. With that he gave us the 100-watt smile. I gave him the smile back and, just for the hell of it, I waved at him with the bandaged hand. That might give him something to think about. Why was I waving with that hand? Was I left-handed? Was it some kind of message?

As suddenly as the warmth had been put there it was wiped away. He bent over his papers. But somehow, some way I'd missed, a signal had passed from him to the maître d' and brought him hurrying over to Jocko's table. It wasn't a really long conversation. Maybe fifty words but Jocko did all the talking. The maître d just jerked his head a few times. He hurried away and came back with a pot of coffee. He filled Jocko's cup and bowed himself out of range.

"You think it takes that long to ask for a cup of coffee?"

Hump shook his head and got up from the table. I knew he'd gotten the hint and taken off after the maître d', doing his best to look like he was on his way to the john. He followed the maître d' past the cash register and into the main dining room. While I waited I signaled our waiter and ordered a carafe of chablis for me and one of burgundy for Hump. I was sipping the first glass of mine when Hump came back. He sat down across from me and shook out a cigarette and lit it from an open book of matches he had in the palm of one hand. He passed the pack of cigarettes across to me with the open book of matches. I lit one of his and read the number in the inside of the book.

?74-2032

"I was one step too far behind him," Hump said.

I pushed the cigarettes back across to him and kept the matches. "The question is how many phone numbers in Atlanta have these same last six digits?"

"Lord knows." Hump poured himself a glass of burgundy. "Maybe Art would know."

I left the table and retraced Hump's movements toward the men's room. There was a bank of three pay phones near the entrance to the rest rooms. I dug out a dime and dialed the department number.

"Is that all you've got?"

"It might be something," I said, "and maybe not."

"Hell, he's probably ordering another number ten can of tomato paste."

"It might lead us to Charleston," I said.

"Who used to do your scud work before you knew me?" But he said he'd do all the checking he could and if I'd call back in half an hour or so he'd let me know which grocery store Jocko shopped at.

"Addresses, too," I said.

Art grunted and hung up.

"These are the possibilities." We were eating the antipasto and I had to stop long enough to get rid of a ripe olive pit. "One—the call doesn't concern us. In that case nothing to sweat over. Two—the call was to Beck. We've made him nervous and he wants his shadow around."

"Easy enough to check out," Hump said. "We'll know when the door opens and in walks Beck."

"Yeah, and that might mean all we've got is the last six digits of Beck's home phone."

"A waste then."

"The one I'm hoping for is that the call is to Charleston, telling him we're here. Or if Beck's with Charleston it could be to Beck at Charleston's number."

"So if Beck walks in we really don't know what's waiting out in the parking lot?"

"Either someone or no one."

"That's a help."

We went on eating the antipasto.

I'd checked my watch when the maître d' left to make his call. Twenty-three minutes later the outside door opened and a man walked in. Hump saw him and nodded at me.

"Beck," he said under his breath.

Watching him as he moved down the aisle toward Jocko's table, I had a hint of a feeling why Art and Hump had been impressed by him. He moved like a ballet dancer with balls. And when he took off the light tan camel hair coat, I saw that he probably had been a boxer at one time. He had the shoulders and the arms for it. The cut of the suit didn't hide it. He had the flat, hipless and almost rump less body and the short legs that seemed out of proportion to the rest of him.

"Art strikes out on that. No can of tomato paste."

Hump nodded.

Beck sat across the booth table from Jocko. He listened for a minute or so and then he turned slowly as if looking for the waiter or the maître d', but the real purpose was that long look at us. The eyes studying us had the flat glassy look of beads used as doll's eyes.

"He know you?" I asked Hump.

"He knows me. Curled his lip at me for a kiss."

"What happens now?" I asked.

"Two beautiful hunks of trim come in, sit with us, play with our knees and then run off with us. And when we're all in the same bed naked, in walks Charleston and puts a monogrammed knife in each of us."

"Sounds like fun," I said.

"I hope they let us get a little before the knife part of it."

My scampi came and Hump's huge platter of spaghetti and meatballs. I adjusted my napkin and looked down at the shrimp. "I think it's their move. Maybe it'll be a bad one."

Hump plopped a meatball in his mouth and grunted.

While the waiter poured the coffee, I got up and went around to the deck of phones. Art was waiting for my call.

"Hell of a lot of combinations possible. I had them checked out. We eliminated most of them. Phones that had been in the name of the same person for years. Business phones. Cut it down to three. One was a church so I threw that one out. I might be wrong but I'd pick this one. New phone installed on Tuesday, the day after the J.C. Cartway fight. I reached the man who installed it at home. Says he can remember it because the whole house was empty. A house on Piedmont Road." Art gave me the number.

"He says nobody was there when he installed the phone. A note on the door telling him where they wanted it installed. Nothing in that room but a cot bed."

"How's it listed?"

"Hold onto yourself. Charles Tree."

"Our boy," I said. I edged around and saw Beck approaching. He seemed unaware of me, just moving toward the john. "Doing anything about it?"

"Going to stake the place out. Got a man out there now finding us a room or an apartment across the street."

I kept my eyes on Beck as he seemed to head directly toward me and then swerve at the last minute and go into the restroom entrance. "Can't you just tear the goddamn door down and go get him?"

"Get who? I'm not even sure it's Charleston. I'm not even sure anything wrong's going on over there."

"Who owns the house?"

"We're checking that now."

"You're a big help," I said.

"You are, too," Art said. "You remember Uncle Walter?"

I did. The candy-assed head of our section.

"He's very impressed with me. Wants to know where I'm getting all this good information."

"And you said. . . ?"

"I told him I had a new informer," Art said.

"Thanks a lot." I waited a second. "Call me at home if anything breaks. I owe him and I'd like to be around."

"All informers get paid," Art said, laughing before we broke the connection.

It was slow in the other room. I drank my coffee and told Hump about the house on Piedmont Road. He heard me out and then tipped his head toward Jocko's table. "Nothing out here. I think this visit, except for the phone number, might be as big a zero as the Braves."

"It's like chess," I said. "Never learned to play it. Never learned the rules. Used to watch a couple of guys at the department play it during their lunch hour. It didn't make any sense at all. Maybe because I didn't know the rules."

Hump looked puzzled. "It might be the wine, but I'm having trouble following you."

"I'm having trouble following myself. I think I'm walking around the point of it, if there was a point. Just this—the one thing I learned about chess was that there were pawns and they were expendable and you gave them up for other advantages. And then there were queens, kings, knights and bishops and you were careful with them. Didn't waste them."

"A class system of sorts," Hump said.

"Now us here. Things are happening. Vibrations and static but we don't know how to take them. The big thing is that we don't know how they see us."

"Pawns," Hump said.

"If so, then they know we just blundered into this and our only involvement in it is that we're stepping on corns. Getting in the way."

"Kings, queens, knights or bishops," Hump said.

"Then we're on the kill list."

"You're cheerful," Hump said.

There was movement in the corner of my eye. I looked around and watched as George Beck left Jocko's booth and cut across the aisle toward our table. Up close his eyes looked as hard and glassy as they'd seemed from a distance. He stopped about three paces away.

"Mr. Giacommo wants to know if you'll have a drink with him." Beck's voice had a strange quality, the New York harshness and flatness softened to a degree by a dash of Southern speech.

"What about it, Hump? You want to have a drink with Mr. Giacommo?"

Beck cut in before Hump could answer. "The invitation's just for you. Not the shine."

Hump moved slow and easy, not a jerk to it, until he was looking up at Beck. When he spoke he was still facing Beck, but talking to me. "Go ahead and have a drink with the fat spic if you want to, Jim. It's no red off my candy."

I shook that off. "Tell Jocko …," I began.

"Mr. Giacommo doesn't like to be called that," Beck said.

"Tell Jocko I didn't come here to be insulted by the hired help. I don't need a drink that bad."

Hump grinned up at Beck.

Beck said it flat, all the softness gone, back in the New York streets, "You and me, shine, you and me."

"Just as long as you don't kiss me before I know you better," Hump said.

"You've killed a few men, haven't you, Jim?"

Hump knew the answer. He'd been there one time, the night when I'd had to chop Eddie Spence when I hadn't wanted to. When I'd hesitated he'd been yelling at me to burn him before Eddie got lined up on me. So it was a question leading somewhere. "A few," I said.

"I haven't."

Across from us Beck was carrying the message back to Jocko. Jocko's eyes played across us and moved away.

"Better you don't," I said.

"Never wanted to before. A few good licks and my mad's gone. Up to now. But Beck's got me going in the wrong direction."

They'd finished talking across from us. Jocko, slowly, almost kingly, stood up and came toward us. He stopped next to my elbow and waited until I looked up at him.

"We seem to have a misunderstanding, Mr. Hardman. I assure you I had no intention of insulting your friend, Mr. Evans."

"The message got garbled."

"Mr. Beck grew up in a rough part of New York and he has an unreasonable hatred of blacks."

"His problem," I said. "Ought to keep it at his house."

Jocko nodded and smiled. "I'd still like to have that drink with you … and with Mr. Evans."

I waved toward a chair. As soon as Jocko started to sit, Beck got up from the booth and took a step toward our table. "But I don't want to drink with your Mr. Beck. I can be unreasonable, too."

Jocko hesitated just an instant and then turned and waved Beck away. Beck returned to the booth, but he sat on the other side, in Jocko's seat so he could watch us.

The maître d' trotted over and hovered near Jocko's elbow. Jocko paid him no attention at all. "I have some excellent thirty-year-old cognac."

"Fine with me," I said.

The maître d' sprinted away. As soon as he was gone, Jocko spread his hands and gave me his best apologetic smile. "I hope you won't be offended by what I have to say, Mr. Hardman. I have, of course, done some checking on you. I know you were an honest cop and that you were treated unfairly. I know how you make your living now. I even know about those trips to New York you and Mr. Evans make from time to time and what you bring back with you." He shrugged his shoulders slightly, as if it didn't matter much to him. "I make it my business to know."

"I figured as much," I said.

Jocko's gaze shifted to Hump. "And Mr. Evans is equally well-known. Once, while watching a professional game on TV, I made a thousand dollars by wagering that Mr. Evans would get to the quarterback three times that afternoon. I believe it was against Chicago."

"I think I had one good afternoon against them. Must have been that Sunday."

"It is not a thing I like to admit. You may misunderstand this admission. It may seem that I am trying to buy your good will. Perhaps you won't remember. You were hurt in the game against Dallas?"

"That was the one."

"When you were in the hospital waiting for the knee operation, you received a plain white envelope with ten new hundreds in it. No note, not even a paper clip."

"I remember."

"You may wonder why I've told you all this. I'd like you to believe that is because I have your interests at heart." He looked from me to Hump, trying to read our faces. He broke it off when the maître d' arrived with the bottle of cognac and three over-sized snifters. Jocko waved the maître d' away and poured it himself.

"Go on to what's on the bottom line," I said.

Jocko passed the snifters around. I held mine in my good hand and warmed it. Jocko looked down at his, swirling it around in the large glass bowl.

"You seem to be a blunt man, Mr. Hardman. Very well, we can dispense with the dressing. I have some advice for both of you." He put his nose over the rim of the snifter and breathed deeply. Then he tipped the glass and poured a small swallow onto his tongue. He took a long time to swallow it. "The advice is this. You are now involved in something that does not concern you. It is a dangerous business and the end is already known. It is as well-known as if it happened last year. Nothing you can do will change that. I suggest that Puerto Rico is nice this time of year. If you go to the Adams Travel Agency in the morning, you will find first-class tickets reserved and prepaid waiting for you. In San Juan there will be reservations at the Ocean Cabana, a suite. Unlimited funds will be available to you. Stay there for two weeks, rest and acquire a tan." He stopped and gave Hump an apologetic smile. "At the end of that time this business will be finished."

"Tempting," I said.

"We are men of the world, not priests or Sunday school teachers. The fact that you are here means that you know or have guessed some connection I may have with the events of the last few days. I am willing to let that pass. A guess is one thing, a fact is another." He took little cat sips of the cognac, waiting for me to speak, eyes on my face.

"It sure is tempting," I said.

"Sleep on it tonight. The tickets will be there until noon tomorrow. If they haven't been picked up by then, I will know that it was not tempting enough."

I nodded.

"It has been a pleasure talking to both of you." Jocko pushed back his chair and stood up. He turned me off, as if I didn't exist anymore for him. He had one last thing to say to Hump. "Mr. Beck has taken a rather strong dislike to you for some reason, Mr. Evans. I would suggest that you not push your luck with him. He can be ... unreasonable."

At first I wasn't sure that Hump would answer him. The silence went on and on. Perhaps Jocko knew more than I did because he waited. "All this polite shit aside," Hump said, "if you turn him loose on me you'd better order his replacement from Sears and Roebuck."

"I don't think I'll quote that to Mr. Beck."

"He's your animal," Hump said. "Do what you want to with him."

Jocko left. The maître d' rushed over and got his snifter and the bottle of cognac and carried it to Jocko's booth.

"It's getting cold here in Atlanta," I said. "How do you feel about sun and warm sand and all that?"

"I can't tell you. My back's up."

Mine was, too. I waved at the waiter and we finished the thirty-year-old cognac while we waited for our bill.

"A one-day reprieve." We were in my driveway. The engine was idling and the windshield wiper squeaked against a fine frosty rain.

"Or it's a line," Hump said. "Make you think nothing's going to happen and then walk all over your backbone."

"You might as well take my sofa tonight. Hard for anybody to surprise both of us. You carrying?"

Hump reached past me and tipped the glove compartment open. The .38 I'd taken from a drunk and given him was there. "Good by me, but first, I think we picked up company when we left The Gondola. Maybe the head-waiter made another phone call. He pulled up a couple of houses back." Hump brought out the .38 and placed it on the seat next to his hip. "I'm going to take a short drive. I'd like to see if he follows me or stays here. Might tell us something."

"I'll make some coffee."

I got out and walked across the lawn in the fine cold rain. Hump waited until I got the door open before he backed out and headed the way we'd come. The house was empty. I got the .38 from the nightstand beside the bed and put it on the kitchen table while I put the water on. I turned on the radio and got some music. After a couple of songs the news came on. The death of Heddy was the featured story. It was being treated as another of those rape-murders that seem to be a part of the Atlanta crime scene. I guess that was Art's doing. He didn't want Charleston to know that we'd tagged him for it. It was better to let him think that he'd covered his tracks well.

The phone rang in the bedroom. It was Hump. "I'm at the service station down the road. He didn't follow me. That means they're more interested in you."

"What's the car?"

"Blue '71 Fury. I could get the tag numbers. But it's parked in front of the house with the rock fence around it."

"Come on in. The water's boiling."

Art wasn't in when I called the department. I said it was important and the man who took the call said he'd reach Art and have him return the call. I left my number but not my name.

Hump came in a couple of minutes later. "He's still out there. Didn't get a good look at him, but I think it's just one man."

I passed him his coffee. "My guess is he's going to spend a miserable night out there, just on the chance we might lead him somewhere. Jocko's nervous and he wants to know what we do between now and tomorrow noon."

"Sleep," Hump said, "I'm going to sleep."

I was one step from the bed when Art returned my call. I'd reached the point where I felt almost anything that came up could wait until the morning. I was wrong again.

"Got a break," Art said. "The house we've staked out isn't rented, isn't sold and it's supposed to be empty. The owners are in Miami and I had some trouble finding their son. He says the house isn't on the market, that it's supposed to be renovated starting sometime next week."

"So you've got breaking and entering if nothing else?"

"It might not be Charleston. Maybe it's just some cheap con or other. We might end up catching a chicken rather than a hawk."

"When?" I asked.

"Soon. The problem is that we're not sure there's anyone in the house. No car out front and no lights that we can see from over here."

"You might blow it," I said.

"Got to take the chance. If nobody's there we leave it like it is. A look around might tell us if he's flown or might be coming back. I'll be damned if we're going to stake out this place for a week and then find out he's left for good."

"I'd like to go in with you. But I've got a tail out on the street and I wouldn't want to lead him over there." I told him about the blue 71 Fury and gave him an idea of where it was parked.

"Give me fifteen minutes. I'll get a cruiser over there. Have him checked out as a prowler. Drive past the Fury. If the cruiser's there, come straight over. I'll have them check out the car, see if it's stolen, all that crap."

"And if the cruiser doesn't make it we'll have to peel him off ourselves?"

As a last thought before we left the house I got out a flask and poured the last of the calvados in it. It was a cold damp night out there.

When we passed the Fury I could see the cruiser parked behind it and the two cops shaking the car down. We passed it and circled back toward Piedmont Road. Hump found the house without too much trouble. It was a small brick- and stone-fronted cottage set fairly far back from the road. As we passed it and I got a look at the other buildings in the area I understood why the house had been chosen. It was a changing neighborhood, with new apartment buildings clustering around it pushing in at it. If it had been a house in a single-family area, the people in the other houses might have noticed a stranger. Not so with the apartment dwellers. They didn't notice much and they didn't seem to care.

At the end of the block Hump turned and headed back. We parked in the lot next to the Piedmont Apartments and went in. We rode the elevator up to the 6th floor and knocked on the door of 604. The young cop who'd been with Art at the Headhunter Lounge that night, Bill Matthews, opened the door for us. He didn't seem especially pleased to see us. He didn't speak and if he nodded, it got lost in the quick turnabout he did as he headed back into the main room, the living room.

There were three other cops in the living room. All young and all trying to look hard. Art didn't introduce us. From the way they acted and the fact that I didn't know any of them, I made my guess that they were uniformed cops that Art had requisitioned on short notice to make up the stake-out team.

At the front window there were two cameras on tripods. One had the fat magazine of a film camera. The other had a lens that must have had a hell of a focal length. That was for stills. But all that was out the window now. Art had an excuse for going in and there was little chance they'd get used.

Art came over and offered us coffee. We took it and offered him a spike from the flask. He put his back to the others and covered me while I tipped the flask and let a bit run into his cup.

"Trouble with the tail?"

"Good timing all around," I said. "What are we waiting for?"

"You and for two more cruisers to work their way over here. I want us covered in case he's there and slips away from us somehow."

I looked at the three young cops. "How'd you explain me?"

"Said you were a friend of the owner. That you came over to see if the house'd been damaged any."

"They believe you?"

"Not much."

The phone rang then and Art answered it. He listened and said a few words and hung up. "It's on. They're in place." He held his hand out to Bill Matthews. "You got the house key?"

Matthews handed him the key. He looked at Hump and then at me. "You sure you don't want me along?"

Art shook his head. "You've got the number over there. You see anybody coming, you ring it twice and hang it up. If anybody gets surprised it better not be me."

Matthews still didn't like it but he didn't argue. I guess they'd been training them better since my time, since the time Art and I had been coming up.

❧ ❧ ❧

The three young cops went down in the elevator with us. One of them, at a sign from Art, peeled off and took his station across the street from the cottage. It would be his job to back it up if anything went bad. He was also near the radio so he could alert the cruisers if they got past him.

The other four of us crossed the street and followed a curving walk up to the cottage.

"You carrying?" Art asked.

"Maybe," I said.

"Don't use it unless it's tight."

"Not unless he cuts me again."

"Oh, shit, I know you've got some sense." Art tipped his head toward Hump. "How about him?"

"I think so."

Art lowered his voice. "I've got to take the young one with me. Just in case he blows. You and Hump'll have to take the back door." He touched my arm. "Watch yourself."

I dropped back and waited for Hump. I tapped him on the shoulder and we cut across the lawn and headed around the side of the house. Away from the street lamps it was suddenly dark. I stepped over a low picket fence and we were in the backyard. No light from the house that I could see. I found the back door, up some brick steps to a screened-in porch. That meant there was one more door, one from the porch into the house. I didn't like that. Still, I didn't want to run the risk of making noise entering the porch. A squeaking screen door hinge or a loose board on the porch might blow it all.

I took a quick look around the yard. There wasn't time to figure it that close. I pointed over to a picnic table under a large oak about twenty yards away from the door and to the side. Hump made it in about six quiet steps and took his position in the shadow of the oak. As soon as he was in place, I flattened against the porch and squatted near the steps. I was out of the porch sight lines but close enough to jerk his legs out from under him if he came barreling out at the run.

It was a short wait. I heard a lock snick and the back door opened. I brought the .38 up to the ready. The steps across the porch were slow. It was Art. "He's gone, Jim. Come on in, but take a deep breath of good air. It's not pretty in here."

CHAPTER NINE

L ike the man said, it wasn't pretty. We were in the one furnished room, if you could call a cot bed and a telephone on a
chair furniture. It was probably one of the bedrooms in the house
plans. There was a small bathroom off to one side with a low-watt
bulb burning in it.

The cot looked like it'd been used for major surgery. If
there'd been a pillow and sheets, they were gone now. The thin
mattress might have been painted red-black but it hadn't. It was
dried blood and the room was full of the stench of it.

I crossed the room and pushed up a window. Hump followed me and stood behind me, taking in some long, shud-
dering breaths of the chill night air. When I had my stomach
back in place, I got out the flask and passed it. The young cop
got it first because I saw that he needed it the most. He looked
about ready to vomit and his hand shook when he tipped the
flask back.

"No body?" I had my sip and passed it to Hump.

"Unless it's in the backyard or they carried it away."

"Or the cellar," I said.

Art took the flask and shook it near his ear. "You think he's
coming back?"

I rounded the bed and looked at the phone. The message was
there. The cord was ripped out of the wall box. I indicated it to
Art and he nodded and then had his drink. "He's flown."

"He had his fun. But he crapped in his nest. He's gone to find
him another one."

Art sent the young cop over to room 604 to pass the word. He wanted a crew on the double, including lights and shovels. The young cop left looking like he'd just won the Irish Sweepstakes, that happy to be away from the operating room.

"You want to make a guess who this blood belonged to?"

"Maybe Fred Maxwell," I said. "We know Charleston was looking for him."

Art pointed at the cot. "Why all this?"

"Fun and information. He wanted some names... if it was Maxwell he worked on."

"I want some information myself."

"I'll have to make a call. After that, maybe you'll get it. Fair enough?"

"It is if I get the information."

Hump and I crossed the street and went up to room 604. I dialed Annie Murton's number and waited. From the time it took her to answer, I guess she'd been asleep. I explained the situation to her, how it was going sour and I thought it was time to unload what we knew on the police. Annie didn't like that. Maybe she'd let herself believe that Hump and I could cover for the kid, Edwin. That we'd bring him home unhurt and she'd spank him and put him to bed without supper. I had to get her past that so I put it hard and nasty. How Heddy had died and now the bloody cot bed across the street. "I think Edwin's still alive but the time's running. Unless we get to him fast he's dead, dead, dead."

I'm glad it was a phone call because I think she must have cried then. I'm glad I didn't have to watch it. It was a measure of the kind of strength she had that she choked it back. "If you think it's best, Jimmy."

"I do."

"Tell them then. And you'll stay on it?"

I said I would and I said I was sorry I'd been rough. She said she understood and we said goodnight.

Art met us at the door of the cottage. "We don't need the shovels after all. Down in the basement."

We followed him inside. "Who is it?"

"I don't know." He looked at Hump and then at me. "I thought you two might do an I.D. for me."

Hump shook his head. "Had enough blood tonight."

He stayed in the front room. I followed Art through the halls and down the narrow stairs into the basement. It had the smell of damp earth and there was a single bulb burning near a furnace. Art handed me a flashlight and nodded in the direction of a dark corner in the far left.

I played the light across the body once. That was enough. I swung the light away. The vomit bubbles were breaking in the back of my throat. It was that nasty a cutting job.

"Maxwell?" Art asked when I handed the flashlight back to him.

I shook my head, still not able to answer. I choked and swallowed and then I could talk. "Not Maxwell." I went up the stairs and Art dogged me. "An actor. I don't know his name."

That meant the hunt had caught up with us. Charleston knew about the kids from the Burger Shack. And maybe if the old actor had been holding back something he knew from us, then Charleston was in the clear and moving beyond us. The way the old actor looked now he hadn't been able to hold back anything.

Art and I stood on the back porch and I laid it all out for him, point by point. When I finished Art hawked and spat a big glob into the screen where it hung there, some of the feeling he had about me for holding out on him for that long.

The old actor's name was Hardy Simpson. We got that from the wallet in the bundle of clothes we found under the stairs in the basement. There was a ring of keys too and Art followed us in his car and we showed him the way to Tindall Place.

I found the tagged keys to the boys' apartment and Art went over to look around while Hump and I remained in Simpson's apartment. There wasn't that much to see, but I wasn't sure I wanted to sift through the wreckage in apartment 3 again. Once had been enough. While Hump prowled the other rooms, I stopped to read some of the playbills the actor had arranged on one wall. He'd been Mercutio in a 1943 production of *Romeo and Juliet* at the Town theater in Columbia. He did the 3rd Guard in a 1959 production of *Antigone* at Richmond. One season, 1963, he'd been the house manager with the Barter Theater. In between he'd been in some crowd scenes with *The Lost Colony*. The most recent one was dated back in 1969 when he'd been Charlie Horse in a production of the Atlanta Children's Theater. In something called *Animal World*.

"In here, Jim."

I found Hump in the kitchen. He was standing next to the sink. On the drain board there were two thin-stem glasses. They were on a paper towel and there were still beads of moisture on the glass and a damp ring on the paper towel. On the kitchen table there was about half a bottle of Strega.

Two glasses. That meant Charleston had probably come by to check on the boys. He'd pretended some interest in the old actor, maybe been a little fey with him. They'd had a drink of Strega and Charleston had suggested that Simpson go over to his place for a drink. I could see the old actor jumping on that hook.

But Strega? That was like drinking perfume.

We found Art in the living room of apartment 3. He was sitting on the sofa and shaking his head. "How do you figure this?"

"The way it looks," I said.

Hump stepped over to the pile and kicked into it. "That old actor, those playbills, they give me an idea. This place looks like a goddam stage set. Curtain comes up and somebody says it looks like somebody tore the place up and left town."

Art wasn't much interested. "What else does it say?"

"I'm beginning to feel they never left town. That they just staged this so we'd think so."

"You think the old actor knew?" I asked.

"Maybe. Maybe not."

Art grunted. "It's good talk but short on proof."

"Come on, Art. Open your head. Why go to all this trouble? They did this the morning after the robbery. That's hours before they're blown, hours before Charleston comes to town, hours before Jake gets this throat cut."

"All right ... why?"

"One of these kids has a cute mind on him. This is just in case it goes sour. This is thinking ahead. They do this charade and they con the old actor and then they load up the van ... and drive across town." Hump looked at me to see how I was reacting.

"Maybe," I said. "At least if we look for them here in Atlanta we can sleep in our own beds at night."

"I'm not through yet. Look at it this way. If you want to leave town and you don't want anybody to know, if you want a few days head start, you just walk out of the house like you're going out for a beer and you keep going. No goodbye to talkative old actors. No tearing the shit out of the place like this. Just walk out and nobody knows you're gone. Two or three days before they get over thinking they've just missed you coming and going."

"Or you tell everybody you're leaving and you really leave town," Art said.

"And go to all this trouble? Shit, man, it must have been hard work tearing up this place."

"It's worth checking around," I said to Art.

Art nodded reluctantly. "I guess so."

"If Charleston's still in town, they're still in town," Hump said.

"I wonder where that bastard's sleeping tonight," I said.

"If he's sleeping at all," Hump said.

We left Art sifting through the old actor's things. Not that he expected to find anything worth the trouble. It was just a thing some cops did when they couldn't decide what the next step was.

What do you do for a living? the girl asked him.

They were in the oversized bathtub on the second floor. The girl was the one they called Kitty, a dark-haired girl who was probably 19 or 20 but she had the hard, underdeveloped body of a 13-year-old. Most of her regular customers were in their fifties, men who needed almost the spice of perversion to get them up. After the afternoons with the tired, the sick and the flabby, this man was almost too much to believe. Kitty wasn't supposed to ask personal questions. The johns had first names and that was all. But this man had touched some animal part deep in her and she couldn't fight the compulsion to know more about him.

I sculpt, the man said.

What?

I'm a sculptor, the man said.

Oh, an artist?

Yes.

You mean shapes, like the rusting metal thing in front of Colony or the concrete things in Peachtree Center? Kitty asked.

No, the man said, forms. Human forms.

The girl lifted her hands over her head in a pose she'd seen somewhere. The nipples on the small, child-like breasts were like dark raspberries. Would you like to sculpt me?

No, the man said. His hands, smooth and hard as good shoe leather, cool like stone, caught her under the arms and lifted her. No, I have other things I'd rather do with you.

"Something else occurs to me," Hump said as he drove me home.

"Another part of your argument?"

"Not that. It's that call the headwaiter made at The Gondola."

"What about it?" I asked.

"The call's made. Twenty minutes or so later Beck comes in. The call was made to the number on Piedmont Road. It might be that Beck sat around and watched while Charleston cut the old guy up into beef jerky."

"That's a bad thought to hold in your head," I said.

"Isn't it?"

I left the phone off the hook and we slept until noon.

CHAPTER TEN

Exactly at one-thirty I parked in the lot next to the boarded-up empty auto parts store. That was the cover for the fancy, expensive apartment The Man had put in the loft area above. He was a black man who'd made it the hard way. He'd started out as a pimp and in a short time he'd taken large chunks of most of the rackets in Atlanta for himself. The money you paid for that grass you bought from a beard down in the tight squeeze area ended up in his pocket. That doll of a black girl who ran into you in front of a nightclub while you were trying to flag a cab and said, "I'll do it for thirty-five" probably worked for him. And there were the hard drugs, the books, and the numbers.

I'd called him while Hump and I were having breakfast. He said it was a bad day for visitors, a business day, but if it was important he could see us for a few minutes right at one-thirty. That's why we were there exactly on the dot. Since the try on his life, the one we'd helped protect him against, it wasn't easy to get past the outside entrance. If I knew the new safeguards there'd be a man at the door waiting for our knock, one hand on iron while he watched the sweephand on his watch.

Before the echo of my knock died out, the door was opened by a slim young black. He was a new one, one that hadn't been around when the hard stuff was going on last December. He looked us over, shoulders and hips, before he opened the door wide enough and motioned us in. "Any iron?"

"Neither of us," I said.

He waved us up the stairs and followed us. One of the last times we'd been in this stairwell there'd been a dead black man at the foot of the stairs ... one of The Man's bagmen ... and at the top, on the landing, there'd been a dead white man, a contract man from out of town.

The Man was at the table in the kitchen area. That was at the back of the room we'd entered, beyond the living room and the big circular bar with its showy display of booze. The second he heard us enter, The Man slapped the covers closed on two Samsonite briefcases and clicked the locks in place. He came to meet us but he didn't offer to shake hands. The smile he gave us was frosty around the edges. We'd helped him but he hadn't been able to forgive us the way we'd done it. We'd said some hard words to him in front of the help and we'd manhandled some of his friends.

"Have a seat," he said in that learned-late-in-life precise way he had of speaking. "Would you like some coffee?"

"Already had too much," I said. Hump shook his head.

The Man made a thing of tipping his head to look at my bandaged hand. "I heard about your encounter with the blade."

"My question is—how does the other guy feel?"

"A bruise," The Man said, "no damage that mattered."

"Too bad."

When he didn't say any more I knew the prelims were over. It was time to talk if we were going to talk.

"Is Charleston still in town?"

"He was yesterday," The Man said.

"And today?"

"It is hard to say."

"How can I find out?" I asked.

"You can stand in one place long enough and you'll know." He nodded toward the bar. "Is it late enough in the day?"

"I think so."

"Scotch if I remember correctly." The Man motioned to the slim young black. "J.M.'s new with me."

J.M. ducked under the bar and asked how we wanted it. I said over the rocks would be fine for both of us. He mixed a hard shot for each of us.

"You see," The Man said after we had our drinks, "Charleston does not like you very much, Hardman. He fancies himself a ladies' man and if that kick of yours had been an inch or two higher you might have ruined one of his pleasures."

"We know about his other pleasures," I said.

"His work with the knife?" The Man nodded. "If I were you I would consider a trip to San Juan."

"Too late," I said. "The offer ran out an hour and a half ago."

"I could reinstate it for you with one phone call."

"I don't think so. Hump and I have business in town."

"Then you have wasted my time. The Charleston man will be by to see you when he is ready." He looked at me with that same frosty smile. "I assume you only wanted to know if Charleston had left town for good?"

"I want him on my own terms," I said. "Today or tomorrow at the latest. This town's getting too bloody for me."

"Jake and the whore? No great loss there." The Man crooked his finger at J.M. and J.M. ducked under the bar and brought him a small snifter of Benedictine.

"There's one more. An old actor who wasn't involved. Operated on like Charleston was a butcher making beef stew meat." I took a sip of the Scotch and tried to shake the image out of my head. "Wish you could have seen it. It'd make a vegetarian out of you."

A touch of distaste crossed The Man's lips and was gone. "I have heard stories that he has learned to like his work too much."

"He loves it. He's over the edge."

"That may be," The Man said. "But I fail to see how this concerns me."

"I wanted to think better of you," I said.

"It can be very dangerous to mix in this."

"He's not going to make it," I said. "That's my promise."

"And you're going to stop him ... with one good hand?" The Man looked at me like I'd gone light in the head. "I thought you were more sensible than that."

"I'm not going to duel him."

"That will disappoint him," The Man said. He looked at his watch and then at J.M. "Would you wait by the outside door. I do not want our other visitors to meet these visitors."

"Yes, sir," J.M. said.

"If any show up, have them come back in fifteen minutes. By then these guests will have run out of tiresome questions."

J.M. went out and closed the door behind him. The Man waited a few seconds, until he was sure that J.M. had moved down the stairs. "You know, I think, that I have no special liking for either of you."

"I figured as much," I said.

"Got the message some time back," Hump said.

"And yet you seem to have some mistaken idea that I owe you something."

"I never said that." I looked at Hump and gave him a wink that The Man let get past. "It might be that you feel you owe us but I never said I felt you did."

"Some people place a high value on their lives and their businesses, other people don't," Hump said.

"I know one thing that only one or two people in the city know. I know where Charleston spends some of his afternoons."

"And you're not going to tell us?"

"I'm not sure," The Man said. "I'll tell you this much. A young lady I know works as a maid at one of those breakfast and lunch houses. Do you know the ones I mean?"

"No."

"They are daytime whorehouses. The businessman or the married man finds them especially useful. The businessman takes a client there for lunch. A married man who can't find an excuse to get out after dark can always find an hour in the morning or in the afternoon. It's a very class place. Top drawer, they say. The hours are, I believe, from ten in the morning until five in the afternoon." Now that he had our attention he held us a moment while he lit a cigarette. "The young lady owes me a favor or two. Just in passing the other afternoon she mentioned that a certain two gentlemen have been buying the whole house after hours for the last day or two. One of the men you know … a George Beck. She didn't know the other one. He's slim, blond, doesn't like to be seen. He called each afternoon before coming, to be certain that the other customers have left."

"It might be," I said.

"Of course, the young lady does not know what she knows. Therefore, that information cannot be traced to me."

"I'd like the address," I said.

The Man ignored that. "Whether Charleston is human or inhuman is no concern of mine. However, I did feel that the robbery was not a well-conceived one in terms of the risk."

"Five young kids did it. The police know who they are. They'll be caught." I drank off the last of the Scotch and put the glass on the bar.

"I'm not sure I approve of that kind of justice any more than I approve of Charleston's way." He sighed and shook his head. "The address of this particular house is 1122 Bricker Road."

I got out a scrap of paper and wrote it down. "You need an intro?"

"Just money. And … you will be very careful that the girl who is a friend of mine does not get in the way of a stray bullet?"

"Even if I have to pass him up," I said, nodding.

"On your way out you might seem somewhat angry at me. I think I can trust J.M. but it will not hurt to cover myself."

"Thanks," I said.

He let us reach the door before he stopped us. "Are we even now, Mr. Hardman?

"If I stop him we are. If I don't stop him I'm going to be too dead for it to matter."

On the way down the stairs and going past J.M. at the door we badmouthed The Man so much that I thought J.M. might be tempted to try one or both of us. Hump was calling him a dumb shit and I said that my big regret was that I'd spoiled that try on him last year. The way J.M. reacted I think it was one of our better performances.

"Today?" Hump was headed through the main part of town. We'd decided not to call Art. We were going to wake him anyway and it might be better to give him the extra few minutes of sleep that a call before we went over would take from him.

"It's not the best move." If we wanted to be sure of Charleston it would be better to catch him out of doors, to take away from him the kinds of games that he could play out of sight behind doors and walls. We wanted him between the car and the house. But it was after two and that gave us less than three hours to set it up and make it foolproof. That wasn't enough time. I knew Art would say that. I was right and he'd be right. What hurried me was that Charleston had put in his day rooting and he was moving well. As far as the five kids were concerned, I wasn't sure that I could afford to give him another day.

"Risky, huh?"

"But it might work."

"And Beck might be there," Hump said.

Edna let us in and kissed me and asked about Marcy. she didn't want to wake Art. She said he'd had so little sleep lately. It turned out she didn't have to. Art came stumbling out of the bedroom in his underwear, red-eyed and needing a shave. "What's this uproar out here?" Edna shadowboxed him back into the bedroom and a minute or two later we could hear the shower going.

Edna came back a little later. There were big spots of water on her house dress and I had a feeling Art had been a little amorous and had tried to pull her under the shower with him. Just by being there we'd ruined it for them. Sad, because when you're my age and Art's you never get back the ones that get away.

Fifteen minutes later we were in the kitchen and Art knew what we'd found out from The Man. And I'd told him what I wanted to do.

"It won't fly," Art said.

"It's that way or not at all."

"That hand," Art said. "Charleston hears a man with a bandaged left hand was there and you can whistle long and hard for him. He's gone."

"Thought of that." I worked the tape free and began to peel off the gauze. It piled up at my feet before I got down to the pad and pulled that aside. The edges of the cut were jagged and crusty, the stitches so tight you could almost play a tune on them. "You got some gauze and tape?"

I left the pad in place and exchanged the heavy padding of the bandage for a small wrapping. I held out a hand to Hump and he passed me the left glove from a pair we'd bought at a sports store on our way across town. It was thin and soft and black, a driving glove. It was some trouble working it over the bandage. I was sweating with the pain and the effort by the time I was through. "There." I held it up. "Lost it in the war."

"Oh, hell." Art got up and poured himself another cup of coffee. "You sure he'll be there?"

"If not today, then tomorrow."

"Hell, you're not even sure he's in town."

I went back over the question-and-answer we'd had with The Man. He'd never said right out that Charleston was in town, but he'd passed the info about the house on Bricker Road. That had to mean something. "My source never said so, but the fact he told me about this at all says Charleston's still here. And unless he's as lost as we are it backs up Hump's theory that the boys are still in town, too."

"If I don't go along with you, you'll cut me out and do it by yourselves?"

"Right."

"This is the silliest sack...."

"Are you in?" I asked.

"I'm in," Art said.

I relaxed then. Hump grinned at me. It was on the way.

CHAPTER ELEVEN

At four that afternoon, wearing a slightly wrinkled suit and a tie that was a shade too mod for me at my age and with a jacket pocket of telephone memo messages ... all fakes ... we pulled up in front of the house at 1122 Bricker Road. We were in a borrowed Continental that I'd talked out of Eddie French who ran one of the local car-leasing outfits.

Number 1122 was a Southern mansion with the big columns and the wide breezy porch that ran the whole length of the house. It was what I'd call *Gone With the Wind* architecture, that is, built after the movie came out and influenced by the movie sets in the same way that some impressionable young girls might have learned their Southern accents from the god-awful one Vivien Leigh had as Scarlett.

Hump was in the front seat. I was in the back. Hump had a kind of rueful look on his face that said he wasn't sure he wanted to be an actor if these were the only roles he could get. He was wearing a black whipcord suit and a chauffeur's cap. The suit didn't fit too well but it was the largest size we'd been able to find on short notice.

"You ready to sit in the kitchen and flirt with the maid while old dad tries out the pleasure of this place?"

Hump laughed. "Hardman, I expect I couldn't finish a cup of coffee before you'd finish your pleasure."

"Ah, hell, who told you?" I grinned at him. "You ready?"

"I'm ready."

"Then how about coming back and opening the door for me? With a deep bow, please."

The young black maid who answered the door was probably The Man's source. She was wearing a short black dress, a frilly apron and one of those white starched things in her hair … whatever you call them. She looked me over carefully, a look that counted the bills in my wallet and the change in my pocket. Then her eyes slid past me and landed, with claws, on Hump who was standing respectfully apart and to my right. It took her an effort to loosen the claws and get back to me.

"Do you have an appointment?"

"He didn't say anything about appointments." I leaned forward and swayed slightly, as if I'd already had a nip or two to get my courage up. "All he said was that you needed to be able to afford it. Is that right or wrong?"

I guess the walk-in traffic was common enough. Also, if she had any doubts about me they didn't extend to Hump. "You can come in," she said to me, "but that gentleman can't."

"My driver, Horace? It's chilly out in the car. At least, couldn't he wait in the kitchen?"

Hump leaned in. "I'd be pleased to wait in the kitchen."

"And he can have two beers on my tab." I put my hard look on Hump. "More than two beers and you're in trouble, Horace."

"Yes, sir. Thank you, sir."

The black maid wasn't sure. "I suppose it's all right." She gave Hump a sad, understanding smile. "But you'll have to go around to the back door."

"I don't mind," Hump said.

As she turned to lead me into the house, Hump cut an eye at me. He could see all the possibilities. There was a chance he was going to have a better time than I was and it probably wouldn't cost anything but a few charming words. In a house where the business was screwing I had a feeling the vibrations even got to the non-screwing help.

Inside the house, after she closed the door, the maid said, "You ought to ask Miss Connie about your man being in the house."

I nodded. We were in a wide hallway that led to a high curving staircase to the left. Straight ahead to the right was the living room. It was in that direction that the maid led me. The living room was furnished as a copy of some article on restoration in some home beautiful magazine. Either they'd bought or rented the house that way or they'd hired some fag interior decorator to put the scene together for them.

A blonde woman in her late thirties was behind a bar to the right of the entrance. She remained there as I crossed the carpet toward her. She wasn't reading my wallet. She was reading the price tags on the clothing. Around two hundred for the suit, a bit over forty for the Florsheim shoes, eighteen to twenty for the shirt, and perhaps twelve to fifteen for the tie. It wouldn't make me her richest customer. It might, however, put me in a class that could afford the $50 or so that was probably the going rate for short-times in the afternoon. On second thought, considering the way they'd wrapped the package, it might be closer to $75.

"Afternoon," she said. The inspection was over. "I don't believe I've seen you here before, have I?"

I shook my head. I gave the rest of the room a lingering, awed look. "A friend told me about it. I thought I'd stop by and see if it was true."

"I'm glad you did." She looked past me and nodded at the black maid. That meant she could leave and that reminded me of Hump.

"My black driver's with me. If it's all right with you I'd like for him to wait in the kitchen. And I said he could have two beers while he waits."

"Of course." The charm was on. The driver gave me a tad more status. I could hear the adding machine chucker-chucker as she wrote off the two hundred dollar suit as an imperfect indication of what I was really worth. But there was a question mark left and I knew that as soon as she got the chance she'd look out to see what kind of car I had a driver for. Perhaps the Continental would satisfy her.

"Now, not more than two beers for Horace," I said to the maid as she left.

The blonde smiled at that. "I'm Connie. I'm going to need some information about you." She reached under the bar and brought out a 3 by 5 file card. "Your first name?"

"Al."

"Your last name?"

"Look," I said with irritation in my voice, "I'm not asking to cash a check. What happens if the police raid this place and find my name and address in your files? How am I going to explain that to my wif. . . . to my company?"

"We don't, of course, plan to be raided."

"Well, my last initial is B and that's as far as I'll go this time." I reached into my jacket pocket and brought out my wallet. I fanned some hundreds at her. "How much?"

Connie tapped the edge of the uncompleted file card with a long polished nail. "That depends. You see, all of my girls are specialists and the price depends upon the kind of special pleasure."

"Well," I lowered my eyes as if I couldn't look at her, "there's one thing my wife doesn't like to do." I let it trail off.

"French then?"

"I guess that's what they call it."

"Seventy-five dollars."

I dug under the "show" hundreds and brought out four twenties. "Will that cover a drink for me and the beers for my driver?"

"Of course." She scooped the twenties from the bar. "Go to the top of the stairs. Room one. Introduce yourself to Melba. She'll know what you want . . . and there's a bar in her room."

I turned and started for the hallway.

"Al?"

I stopped.

She gave me the big smile. "And later, when you're not so nervous, perhaps we can finish filling out our file on you?"

"Maybe."

When I came down the staircase a bit after forty minutes later I'd had two Scotches and the most fantastic demonstration of head that I'd ever encountered. It'd been staged like an exhibition, with mirrors on the side walls and the ceiling and the lights just bright enough to see myself in the middle of it all. At times, caught in the images there, I'd thought I was watching a blue movie rather than being a part of the action. And then, as if she knew, Melba would do something that reminded me that I was very much involved.

I took a long tired breath. The things I go through for my profession. Whatever my profession is. A wry remark that. And then the *triste* hit me and I thought of Marcy and I washed my head of the mirrored images. It was time for business. I'd proven that I was what I seemed, a horny businessman, and now it was open for me to step through the door and find out what I could about the after-hours plans Connie had for the house today.

It was close to day's end. Connie was seated at the bar with her back to me, counting the day's take. From what I could see it must be a profitable operation. When I was a few steps from her, she heard me. It wasn't a hurried thing, but she closed the cashbox and pushed it to one side.

"Was Melba all you expected?"

"More," I said.

She indicated the bar stool beside her. "Are you ready to fill out the card now?"

"If you'll answer one question."

"If I can." But she'd stiffened and it looked like she didn't like questions.

"What are the chances of renting the whole shebang one afternoon, after you close for the day?"

"For just … you?"

"Not exactly," I said. "For me and three of my poker friends."

"It might be worked out."

"How about tonight?" I asked.

"You mean right now?"

"An hour or so," I said. "It'd take that long to get my friends over here."

"I'm not sure. Some of the girls might have other plans. You know, they do have personal lives of their own." She pushed the file card toward me. "Normally we need a day or two's warning before we can put together a special like that."

"How about tomorrow?" I asked.

"I'll have to talk to the girls. If you'll call me tomorrow afternoon I'll let you know. If tomorrow's not a good day we can always find a day that suits all of us."

I filled out the card. *Alfred Burns. Executive Manager. The Howard Company. 432 Marietta Street. Suite 428.* And then I gave her the number of the Baptist Church out near me. Their number was close to mine and I was always getting their calls on hungover Sunday mornings. I handed her the file card and she handed me hers. It was a plain card with just a phone number on it. No name and no address. I put it in my card file and looked around.

"So Melba was fine?"

"Fantastic. Unbelievable." I got up from the bar stool. "Now if I can get my driver, Horace. …"

Connie pressed a buzzer on the other side of the bar. A few seconds later the black maid scurried into the hall and skidded to a stop. Her hands were behind her, struggling with the frilly white apron.

So Hump hadn't been bored at all.

And Connie hadn't asked about my war wound.

⚜ ⚜ ⚜

Hump was standing beside the car, waiting for me. When he saw me come out of the front door he hurried to the passenger door nearest me and swung it open and held it. As he bowed me into the car, he said, "What kept you?"

"Talk, talk, talk," I said.

Hump closed the door and went around to the driver's seat. He kicked it over and pulled out of the driveway. "Who tells first, me or you?"

"Might as well be me," I said. "All that and I drew the blank."

"I did a bit better. The girl, calls herself Francine, got taken with me. Seemed eager to see me again. Even came right out and offered me some of her evenings ... tonight especially."

I nodded on that.

"Now, being somewhat interested in the whole week, I asked about tomorrow. Like tomorrow might be a better night for me. That girl almost cried. Seems she'd said she'd work tomorrow. A private party after regular hours."

"Is it Charleston?"

"A good chance," Hump said. "Without being obvious I got her talking about the place and about those private parties. Something new they just started. Two guys come in and tear up all the stuff in the house. At least one does. The other one does his part and then sits around and smokes and watches most of the time."

"From what The Man says I guess we can assume Charleston does the tearing and Beck does most of the watching?"

"Probably. You see, the way Francine tells it, when these private parties are going on they don't even notice her. She hands around drinks and a joint now and then and she does some cleaning up. Mostly she's invisible. But this one guy wore out the whole damned crew one night, the madame included, and he made a grab for her. It took some running to get away from him. It's not that she's shy but she thinks black is better."

"A description?"

"Same as the others. Slight, blond, five-ten or so. And the last time she saw him he was limping a bit and had a hell of a blue bruise on one thigh."

About a mile from the house we passed the unmarked car with Art and his pick-up crew in it. Hump slowed down and I gave Art the thumbs-down sign. His driver did a u-turn and followed us back into town.

Hump's account of what he'd learned from Francine set it for Art. He was a believer now. I could see him running his mind over the things that could be done to really set it up for tomorrow, now that he had time to do it in a professional way.

"Jim, how are you spending your time until tomorrow?" Art asked.

"The same way I bet Charleston is spending his," I said. "Trying to trace those five kids."

"Where?"

"Where the crap began. With Annie Murton."

"Want me along?" Art asked. "A solid, upright Irish cop might help."

"If you know one bring him along," I said. "Hump?"

"Francine's meeting me a couple of blocks from the house in an hour or so. We'll be at my place all evening. You get something, call me. Especially if Beck's in it."

Before we split from Hump, Art asked, "How was it back there? Worth the money?"

"Me do a thing like that? You know Marcy took my balls with her to Fort Myers in her small change purse."

Art grinned. Beyond him Hump gave me a curl of his lip. One thing about Hump. He knew a cover-up lie when he heard one.

"The Trojan horse," I said, "was really a piece of wet noodle."

"You're holding back on me, Annie." I'd let her do her half hour of back-country politeness and welcome, all I could take, the coffee and the homemade chocolate cake, now it was dark outside and time was running against me. "I know you are, Annie. That kid loves you too much to let you worry. He's been in touch with you and you damn well know it."

"Don't swear at me, Jimmy."

"That's right, Jimmy," Art said with a wry grin at me, "there's no reason to swear at Annie that way."

Annie thanked him. "I guess Jimmy's changed a lot since he was a young boy. At least from what Tippy told me about him he seemed like a nice boy."

"It's not all his fault," Art said. "Jimmy's been under pressure. He took a job trying to help you because you were Tippy's sister and when it looked like the kids had left town, he decided the way to help Edwin was to stop the contract man. That got him cut up and could have gotten him killed."

I looked down at the leather-covered hand, modestly. I'd tried to take the glove off but it had hurt so much that I knew I'd have to cut it off when I had more time.

"Now it looks like the contract man has it figured out. He's ahead of us. I'm not sure how he got there, but it looks like he got some answers out of his victims before he killed them. Anyway, I've got a feeling he's a step behind Edwin and the others and we're a mile behind with blinders on. And, to be as vulgar as Jimmy here, you're not being a damn bit of help."

That got a gasp out of her. It was my turn to push her. "You remember you offered me the whole fifteen hundred as expense money and I only took a thousand. You ever wonder why, Annie?"

"No, Jimmy."

I got out the rest of the roll, what was left from the thousand. It was down to about five hundred now. I put it on the kitchen table. "I figured if it went bad it would buy you a cheap funeral for Edwin. Now it's gone this far, gone this sour, I'm going to turn what's left back to you. You might as well give him a better funeral than the five-hundred-dollar one. Because as sure as we're here drinking coffee and eating chocolate cake, if you know something and don't tell me about it, you might just as well buy the black dress and tell the cemetery to dig the hole."

"I don't want him to go to prison," Annie said.

"Prison's not the worry right now," Art said. "With him on a death list prison might be the safest place for him." But I knew that Art didn't believe that. If they wanted Edwin and the others dead an arm would reach into any prison in the country and get the killing done. But we couldn't admit that to her. Right now we were buying time and worrying about the present death threat rather than worrying about one that might come up in a month or two months.

"If the kids do any time it won't be much," I said. "Most of the money they took was gambling money and I doubt if any of the bookies or gamblers are going to get on a stand and say they were robbed. That's why Charleston got called in. An honest man gets robbed, he calls the cops and the cops catch the robber and the honest man testifies in court and they put the robber away."

Art took it up. "These guys can't work within the system. They can't afford to. They get on the stand and say they were robbed of thousands, then Internal Revenue is going to step in and ask where the money came from."

"Hell, Annie, Art'll tell you there aren't any charges against Edwin or the others so far. For all we know there might never be.

We're after a killer and finding the five kids might be the best way of finding him. If we can get there in time."

"Can I believe you?" Annie asked.

"If you can believe anybody," I said.

"My word I'll try to get him the best break I can," Art said.

She still wasn't quite ready. She left us at the table and went over to the sink. She stood there looking out of the window above the sink. It was dark and I knew she couldn't see anything. I could hear it bouncing back and forth in her, moving her this way and then that. "I guess I'm going to have to trust you," she said finally. "You might be trying to put him in jail but you're not trying to kill him."

"Where is he, Annie?"

"He's at a place called the Dairy. He called me last night so I wouldn't worry."

It turned out that the Dairy was a sort of co-op farm run by an old man who must have been a little out of his head. A group of hippie street kids lived on the farm and took care of a large dairy herd. They made butter and cheese and some of them did leatherwork and dipped candles.

"I've heard of it," Art said. The county police had reason to believe that some grass was grown out there. So far, on the raids they'd made, they hadn't found even a grass seed. The stories, however, kept popping up from time to time.

"Edwin said one of the boys, Henry Harper, knows a girl who lives out there."

I gathered up the roll of expense money and said I'd call her as soon as we knew something. We left her standing at the kitchen table, looking down at the partly-eaten cake and the half-cups of coffee.

CHAPTER TWELVE

O n the outskirts, the fringes of town, the last things we passed
were some auto dealerships and some used car lots and then
the mobile home places all strung with light. We were going south
and it didn't take long to put those behind us. If the moon had
been brighter or we'd done the drive in the daylight, it might have
been beautiful scenery. All the leaves hadn't fallen yet. The stub-
born ones were waiting for the first snap freeze. And all around
us as far as we could see was the farmland, enduring fall, getting
ready for winter and sensing that spring was a long time away.

Hump was in the back seat, eyes closed, not far from snor-
ing, off the far edge asleep. When I'd called him and asked him
to meet us at the department, I'd felt his reluctance. We might
have called at a bad time. He'd had little to say, only some brief
answers to our questions, and he'd said nothing during the drive.

Another half hour driving and Art pulled into a small country gas station and grocery store. I waited in the car while Art
went in to try to get some more exact directions now that we were
close to the Dairy. The light must have bothered Hump. He sat up
and blinked into it.

"We there?"

"Close," I said.

"Wake me when we're closer." He curled on his side and put
his head on the seat.

After another mile or so down the highway, Art turned right
onto an unpaved clay road. We seemed lost and alone then, with
no houses on either side and no lights. Just the silent dark woods.

And then there was a white rail fence that just seemed to appear on our right, not there one moment and then looming up out of the ground the next. We hit a dogleg in the road and followed it and the rail fence was still there, the uneven lines looking like children's chalk lines in the headlights. Up ahead there was a break in the rail fence and when we reached it Art swung left onto a rutted single-car-width road.

I thought I could see lights ahead. I couldn't be sure. We were in thick woods, trashy woods, woods that needed the dead trees cleaned out and some replanting. It was like going into a wood where nobody had been in a long time. And then, in the distance, a dog began to bark.

We broke through the wood and almost before we knew it we were in a compound of some kind. Up ahead we could see the main house, a large farmhouse that might have been the class of the neighborhood some years back, with a wide lower porch and a widow's walk above. Even in the dark I could see that the house had experienced the same kind of neglect that the stand of wood had. Beyond the house and at a distance there was a barn and past those a scattering of small cottages, ones that reminded me of the kind I'd lived in at a boys' summer camp when I'd been eight or nine. There didn't seem to be any pattern to the cottages. They just seemed to be built as the need came up, using the existing land here and there.

There were lights burning in the lower floor of the farmhouse, though the old-type paper roll shades had been drawn down. As far as I could tell there weren't any lights in the cottages. Perhaps it was the religious hour.

"Your move," Art said.

In the back seat, behind us, Hump stirred and sat up.

"How?"

"Talk. I don't have any jurisdiction over the county line. If this goes bad and there's any shooting or trouble, you two are going to have to back me in a lie."

"Hot pursuit," I said.

"Right. That we chased them right over the county line."

"Who?" Hump asked.

"Whoever we have the trouble with." Art looked at me. "You know his grandmother. You've got to talk Edwin, and through him, all of the group into coming back across the county line into Atlanta."

"Talk might not be enough," Hump said. "I've seen the guns."

"That reminds me." Art reached into his coat pocket and brought out a short barrel .38. "A spare. You need it?"

"Yeah." I put it in my right coat pocket and went up to the porch of the farmhouse. I guess that was the choice. Art could go up and say he was a cop and the water pressure all over the county would start dropping where they were flushing their dope. Or I could go up and do some con about insurance. Crossing the porch I fumbled out my wallet and palmed one of the cards.

It was a long wait before they answered the door. It just cracked a foot or so and the light was dim inside. Pouring out of the door toward me was the strong, sweetish scent of incense. The man who looked out at me was the oldest hippie I'd ever seen; He must have been over eighty, scrawny and wasting away. His gray hair was shoulder-length and he wore a tie-dyed shirt that reached to his knees. He was toothless and either he didn't have a set of false or he'd taken them out for the night. "What you want?"

I pushed the card at him. "I want to see Edwin Robinson."

"I don't know anybody that name." He pushed at the door but I'd stuck a shoe there, almost as if by accident.

"Sure you know him." I pushed the card at him again. The way he squinted at it I'd swear he was stoned. "Look, it's no big thing. I've got a check for him. It pays off a claim. Only I couldn't find him and his grandmother say he's out here."

"I don't know any Edwin."

"He's just been here a couple of days. He and four others in a van."

"I don't know their names," he said.

"Are they still here?"

"As far as I know." He pushed at the door and I felt some toes crunch.

"Where?"

"Cabin six."

"Where's that?" I asked.

"After cabin five."

It didn't seem worthwhile to carry that on much longer. I drew my shoe back and let him slam the door. All things considered I guessed I'd gotten as much information out of him as anyone who'd talked to him in the last hour or so.

"You want to arrest an eighty-year-old hippie for dope, that's the place," I said, indicating the house as we passed. Art had moved the car and parked it out of the main compound. Now we were walking past the barn with its heavy scent of manure and cow sweat smell. In the distance we could hear the tinny sound of music from a transistor radio but we could not tell which cabin the music came from. All the cabin windows seemed blacked out for the next air raid, but I guess it was their business if they didn't want people to watch them smoke their dope and do their bedtime trick. Still, a little light might have made it easier for us to read the numbers on the cabin doors.

"Cabin three," Hump said, stepping back.

They weren't numbered consecutively either and we counted our way around the cluster before it hit Hump and he said, "There were two threes." We went back and Hump found a 3 that could have been a 6, as if they hadn't been sure what number they wanted to paint and had compromised with a number that was a cross between them both.

I stepped up onto the porch and worked my way over to the window as quietly as I could. The window had been covered with what had once been a blue plastic shower curtain. The lower right corner hadn't fitted well and I got an eye to that. I couldn't tell if these were the kids we were looking for. There were three of them. Two were standing over an old bed sheet, stripping the leaves from stalks of marijuana and letting them fall onto the sheet. There was a stack of stalks about roof high in the rear right corner they were working from. The third young boy was seated at an old camp table in the center of the room. There was an old wire strainer in front of him and he was cleaning some of the dope. Probably not for sale. Probably for their own use.

I backed off the porch and went over to Hump and Art. I peeled a couple of twenties from the expense money roll and handed them to Hump. It was his move. Everybody knew that blacks liked dope better than whites did. "Make a buy. Find out where Edwin is. Do your stoned black for Art. He's never seen it."

Art and I moved to the side, away from the light when the door opened. Hump clomped across the porch, weaving some as if he'd already had a few lung-fulls.

"Method," I whispered to Art, "he's acting before he hits the stage."

Hump hit the door frame with his hamhand and the windows shook.

There was a long silence and when one of the boys spoke he was close to the door. "Who is it?"

"It's me," Hump said.

"Who?"

"Me. Horace."

"What do you want?"

"I want to see Edwin." When there was no answer right away Hump hit the door frame again. "Come on, open up. I'm not the pigs."

"What?" There was a shake in the voice.

"I said I'm not the pigs. I just want to buy some smoke." Hump hit the door again. "Open the door. If I was the pigs I'd have broke your door down by now."

The door opened slowly. It was the kid who'd been using the wire strainer. He looked Hump over while Hump fumbled around in his pocket and brought out two twisted twenties. "All I want's smoke. And I want to see Edwin."

"He's not here."

"I'm not supposed to buy from anybody else."

"Don't buy then." The kid pushed at the door and Hump hit the door a whack with the palm of his hand that threw it open again. "I'll buy a lid from you and talk to Edwin later."

"You got twenty?" The kid stared out at Hump. Slowly, as if stoned but believing that he was moving at ordinary speed, Hump separated the two twenties. He put one back in his pocket and smoothed the other out by giving it a shoeshine buff across his thigh. "Here's one."

The kid took the twenty and moved away from the doorway. After the experience of Hump whacking the door open I guess he decided that it wasn't worth the trouble. From my angle I could see the part of the cabin that had been blocked from me before. I counted four double bunks on that side. When I saw Hump reach out his hand, I edged back into the shadows. The kid appeared in the doorway and handed Hump a plastic bag. "I didn't weigh it, but it's more than good weight."

"Got a paper?" Hump asked.

"You want to test it?" The kid reached into his shirt pocket and brought out a short joint. He handed it to Hump and struck a kitchen match to give him a light. Hump sucked on it. When he could speak he was choked.

"Dynamite stuff," he said.

The kid grinned at him. "It's the best in the state."

Hump did the courtesy thing then. He took another short hit and passed it to the kid. The kid did his hit like he was sucking an empty glass with a straw, lips popping.

Hump let his breath out slowly. "I got to see Edwin. I know a guy on Ashby wants to make a big buy."

"Edwin's not the big horse here. He just got here."

"The guy on Ashby knows Edwin. Said to be sure and see Edwin." Hump held up the plastic bag. "And to buy a lid to see how the quality was."

"What you think?" The kid turned in the doorway and put his back to Hump, questioning the other two.

"He knows dynamite when he tastes it," one of them said.

The kid in the doorway giggled and the other two laughed with him. That settled it. "You got wheels?"

"Yeah," Hump said.

"Follow that road that goes by the right of the barn. It's about two miles. It's an old tobacco barn. Can't miss it."

Hump backed away. "Thanks for the smoke."

The kid giggled and closed the door.

"All I need," Art said when we reached the car and started down the road past the barn. "Two men with me and one has a bad hand and the other is stoned."

"Not yet," Hump said. "But that lid I just bought is not part of any evidence for a bust. That is dynamite shit."

It was an old wagon road. There hadn't been many cars on the road in a long time. Art drove slowly, trying to keep one set of wheels on the hump in the middle and the other set on the shoulder of the road. It was slow going and we did the last part on low beam. As soon as we could make out the shape of the tobacco barn in the distance, Art cut the engine and the lights. "We walk from here."

We got out of the car and stood looking at the barn. Hump sniffed and moved ahead of us about twenty yards. "Smell that?"

"What?"

"Dust kicked up. Somebody's here before us."

"Another car?" Art asked.

"Probably and not long ago."

"We split," Art said. "Hump, you cover the woods along here. Find the car. If it's the van, stay with it. If it's something Beck or Charleston might be driving, fix it so it won't move. Stay with it in case they sprint off from us."

"All right, but if you see Beck, run him in my direction."

We left him following the shoulder of the road nearest the woods. Art and I cut across into the field. It was a plowed and turned under field. The barn was diagonally ahead of us and there was a weak light inside. Probably a kerosene lamp or two. There hadn't been any electric lines that we saw strung from the direction of the farm compound. And the road had followed the most direct route.

About fifty yards from the barn I tripped over something and fell to my knees. I was lucky and fell on my right shoulder with the left hand up in the air and free. At first I thought I'd tripped on one of the high uneven furrows. Then I thought better of it. It had given a bit too much. Art came over and gave me a hand up. "Your flashlight, Art." I got it and moved back a pace or two. I shielded the light as well as I could. A brief flick on, flick off told me all I wanted to know. A young kid sprawled on his stomach.

Art moved around me and got one of his wrists. "No pulse." He stood up. "Is it Edwin?"

"I don't know." I hadn't bothered to look. If it was, it didn't matter. If it wasn't, then that might be good news for Annie but bad news for the family of some other kid. Somehow there wasn't any consolation in that.

I found I was breathing too hard. I was getting tired of blood. My own and other people's. Maybe it was a sign I was getting too old to cut it anymore but I had an urge to get out the .38 and make a run for the barn.

"Easy, Jim." Art read me and put a hand on my shoulder. "We'll do this the smart way or not at all. If anybody bleeds I want it to be them."

"Name it," I said.

"I think most of these barns were built to the same plan … if there was anything like a plan in those days. A main door … that'll be facing the wagon road. Might be another door or a window at the back. Give me a count of fifty after you reach the back of the barn. I'll be flat against the wall beside the door. If there's a window, break it, a door, give it a kick. Nothing at all, kick the wall. Make some noise and flush them toward me. If they come toward you I'll come in the front door and try to protect you."

"I hope the kids aren't in there."

"That's why I'd rather flush them," Art said. "And watch yourself. There might be one inside and one outside. That's the way I'd play it."

We said our "lucks" to each other and separated.

I got to the rear of the tobacco barn without any trouble. The little trouble there was lay in trying to hit the high sides of the furrows and at the same time keep my eyes moving around the woods nearest to me. The one inside-one outside idea of Art's scared the hell out of me. I knew, if that was the way they'd set it up, exactly which one would be outside. And he had no reason to like me and a few not to like me.

It was a small rear window, probably just for ventilation on those hot days when they racked the stringed tobacco before they fired it. I moved close to the window and listened but there were no sounds from inside. I went on with my silent counting. I reached fifty and reversed the short barrel .38 and, leaning forward, smacked one of the glass panes with the butt. Even as the glass was clattering on the barn floor inside, I was falling away, getting out of the possible line of fire. I'd planned to do it gracefully, to fall on my back and let my rump take most of the shock. But my feet got tangled up in something and I was afraid to run the risk of falling on my right hand and possibly losing the .38. So, at the last minute, I took the shock on the forearm of my left hand. The forearm couldn't take it and the gloved and lightly bandaged hand hit the almost frozen ground. The pain moved like a torch up my arm to my shoulder. Even with the pain I got the .38 reversed and the business end toward the window. About that time two shots reverberated within the barn, in the clay and mortar packing that sealed the joints between the logs. Glass broke in the window and sprinkled at my feet. I used my gun hand to push my way up. Behind me, as the boom of the shots died away, I thought I heard noises in the leaves but they were moving away. Perhaps an animal. At the same time I heard a cry and a grunt around the front of the barn. In the distance something was still running in the leaves and I thought, that's Charleston, but I couldn't go after him. I was probably needed more around at the front of the barn. I made the run around the barn in a wheezing gallop, trying to hit the high points and miss the deep places. I reached the front of the barn with the .38 at the ready and found Art sprawled here in the dim light from the partly opened door. Before I could check him I looked in the barn. Nothing there but huge mounds of marijuana stalks.

I went back to Art and turned him. The only blood I could see was coming out of his nose. It covered his chin and ran down his mouth. Art wasn't out, just stunned.

"Art, you all right?"

His eyes struggled to focus on me. "A fist … and a kick. Think it's Beck. Headed for the car, down the road."

Before I could leave I had to be sure he was able to defend himself. I looked around and found his .38. I put it in his hand. "Watch yourself. Charleston might still be around."

"Get moving." He coughed and splattered blood down his shirt.

"Stay awake." I gave him one more look and took off at a sprint down the road. I was breathing so hard from the run that all I could hear was the thumping of my heart and I might have missed it altogether if the thud and the grunt hadn't been so loud. I turned my head and saw the opening then, where some saplings had been bent and broken. I made a move to follow the opening but caution told me not to and I went past it and made a circle.

About 180 degrees into the circle I broke and edged inward and that was how I reached the clearing. There was just enough light to see the tan Mercury there and as I moved closer I could see Hump and Beck. I brought the .38 but I didn't need it. Hump had George Beck backed up against the side of the Mercury and it was over or it could last another half an hour. Either way the outcome was the same. Hump was driving his fists deep into Beck's belly and ribs and then as Beck would begin to slide Hump would drag him upright. As I watched Hump hit him again in the belly with the right and Beck coughed and spewed vomit all over the front of Hump's jacket. The vomit was in a thin stream and it was hitting Hump all across the chest and arms but he didn't pay any attention to it. He just kept pumping his fist into Beck and I watched it as long as I could and finally I stepped closer and said, "That's enough, Hump."

Hump whirled and for a second I thought he was going to hit me. It was there, on a trigger, ready to spring, but he held it back. It was hard and white hot. I didn't know how it was going to go and then Hump shook his head and mumbled, "He hasn't said it's enough yet." But I think he knew it was because he stepped away and as Beck fell forward, Hump dipped a shoulder and hit him one more time. The fist hit him in the side of the neck and Beck fell on his side and twitched.

The vomit smell up close was overpowering. "He hurt you?"

Hump laughed. "That shit didn't even hear the first one coming."

While we were leaning against the car getting our breath and looking down at Beck, Art came down the road with a handkerchief to his nose. He took in the scene and rolled Beck over onto his stomach and put the cuffs on him.

I shook my head at him. I didn't think that busted bag of bones was going anywhere.

CHAPTER THIRTEEN

Within twenty minutes or so the Dairy was swarming with county and state police. A full search of the area around the tobacco barn turned up no more bodies. For a time I'd been afraid that one or two more of the kids might be sprawled in the field or the woods. From a driver's license we found out that the one I'd stumbled over was Henry Harper, the boy whose father I'd visited the day after Jake's death. The one who was in love with his house. Now there wasn't anything to divide that love. After the funeral he could spend his free time thinking of next year's painting chores, the leaves and pine needles collecting in the gutters and downspouts, a new kind of grass for next year's re-seeding of the lawn.

No trace of Charleston. He'd been too smart to head straight for the Mercury. It'd taken a hothead like Beck to do that. No, Charleston hadn't headed for the car and he hadn't headed for the highway. If he had to, he'd burrow in the woods like a fox and wait us out. The other four kids, Edwin and the remaining three, weren't that smart. Within minutes after Art called the county police, they were picked up on the main highway. They tried to thumb a ride with the patrol car. Art asked that they be brought back to the Dairy for questioning.

We stayed with a tall tale about being in hot pursuit of Beck and Charleston, that we'd followed them across county lines and lost them and then had found them again. The county cop, a man I'd met before and knew to be sensitive about violations of his territory, didn't buy that completely. It had so many holes in it you had to buy it on faith. Still, we'd put a big drug bust in his lap, one he'd been frustrated on for some time, and though we hadn't been able to prevent a murder, we had dropped the murderer or his accessory into the pot as well. It was give-and-take time and the county cop gave a bit. The "give" was that, after Art explained the four kids were wanted in Atlanta as robbery suspects, the county cop agreed to leave a wagon and two men with us while we questioned Edwin and his friends. Afterwards, his men would drive the four kids to the county line and turn them over to our wagon. It might not be to the letter of the law but it was functional.

"Have a seat," Art said.

We were in the farmhouse. It still had the smell of incense clouding it. We'd turned on the overhead lights and we could see why they preferred the dim ones. The living room was a rathole with big dust balls rolling past and cups and dishes here and there. There wasn't any way to guess what had been on the plates or in the cups: mold covered that.

The four kids looked at each other and then walked over and sat hip to hip on the old rump-spring sofa. They were still frightened after the run. Added to that they'd recognized Hump from the rip-off party. He hadn't said anything to them yet but just stood and stared at them. He looked about as mean and rank as he smelled. He'd done some washing up but the sour curse was still on him.

Tight-lipped. That meant they'd make some kind of agreement not to tell anybody anything. The young ones always did that and it often turned out to be a race to see which one'd break first and tell it all.

Might as well start the process. I took a step toward the sofa and picked out the one I was sure had to be Edwin. His startled eyes flicked over me and darted away. "I'm Jim Hardman," I said, "and you must be Edwin Robinson."

"What's it to you, cop?"

"Watch your mouth," Hump said behind him.

"You're Edwin Robinson," I said.

"What if I am?" His chin was up but you could see the quiver built into it.

"Your grandmother's a friend of mine. So's Tippy. I've been working for her, trying to keep you from ending up like Henry Harper out there."

"You're not a cop?"

"Was once," I said "not anymore" and I nodded toward Art. "He's the only cop here."

"How'd you get mixed up in this drug thing?" Art asked.

"We weren't. We'd only been here a couple of days." Edwin was choked but he was getting the words out. They sounded like they came from the mouth of somebody with a broken jaw that'd been wired.

"Shut up, Edwin." The heavyset one with the oily blue-black hair didn't like the way it was going.

"You know how long you can get for being mixed up in growing and selling this quantity of grass?" I asked.

"Ten years if you get a friendly judge," Art said.

"You can do ten years easy," I said. "Of course, the old cons'll probably knock all your teeth out to make your mouth a better cunt."

"They really like nice tight young boys like you four in there," Hump said. "You'll come out thinking and acting like a girl."

"You can be the Andrew Sisters," Art said, "a new female impersonation team."

The wall fell down. At first maybe they thought we'd be satisfied with the information about the grass operation. And they told us about that at great and windy length. At the Dairy everybody who stayed there had to do something to earn their keep. None of the four had wanted to do the milking or the other farm work so they'd agreed to help with the grass cleaning and packing.

After a time we'd had all we wanted of that. It wasn't our interest anyway. It was our way of getting them used to talking. So we shifted gears and pointed at the robbery party after the Cartway fight. That made them hard-lipped again. Hump, who'd had little to say, jumped into the middle of that silence on all fours and kicked it to pieces. It was awesome to watch. How angry he was. How near violence. How close to kicking the shit out of all of them. Who the hell did they think they were anyway? Ripping off seven hundred of his money. Putting a shotgun on him. Pushing him around. Laughing at him, yes, dammit, laughing at him. The money burned him, yes. But the laughing, that was too much. It called for ass-kicking. White-assed kids who couldn't even shave yet treating him like that.

It was all I could do to hold him back. I got a bruise or two doing it. He raved and I talked and I soothed him and he pushed me away and I talked some more. He didn't want to do it. Not a chance in the world. Why, people would laugh at him behind his back if he did. But finally he agreed. He accepted with the reluctance of a virgin whose mother had been badmouthing sex all her life.

"All right, all right," Hump said huffing and puffing, "I'll take my seven hundred and one hundred interest and I won't beat up on your punk kids."

The cache was out in the barn. We stood around and watched while the four of them grunted and sweated their way through two ten-foot high walls of baled hay. Behind that they'd pried off a section of the barn. There, between that inner wall and the outer one, they'd hidden the take. Edwin got the suitcase for me and brought it over. I put it on a bale of hay and opened it. It was the real thing. There was a large cloth sack of watches and rings stuffed in one side of the suitcase. The rest of it was the cash. It looked like they'd had fun counting and stacking it. It was in flat packets tied with rubber bands.

"You counted it," I said to Edwin. "What was the count?"

"A hundred and fifty eight thousand and some odd dollars," he said.

"All of it here?"

"Most of it. We never got to meet with Jake and give him his share."

I took out a packet of hundreds and slipped the band off. I counted out seven bills for Hump and added the eighth that he'd demanded as interest. Art counted with me and watched as I replaced the band and dropped the rest of the packet back into the suitcase.

"All right, you four, follow me." He waited until they were loaded down and started them single-file out of the barn. "Over there to the paddy wagon," he said. At the door he looked over his shoulder at me. "Jim, watch the suitcase, huh?" He marched off after the kids.

"Is Art for real?" Hump asked.

"One way to find out." I grabbed a couple of stacks of the hundreds and tossed them to Hump. I dug out a couple of stacks for myself and then tossed another to Hump. I guessed we'd have carried off half the suitcase if Art hadn't come back, whistling a tune just before he stepped through the doorway. We watched as Art closed the suitcase. "Want to make any bets those kids can't count?" he said.

Art stayed at the city limits just long enough to see Edwin and the others transferred from the county wagon to the Atlanta one that had been waiting. On the way back into town he dropped Hump and me at my house. As soon as he drove away we went into the house and emptied our coat pockets onto the kitchen table. Hump held out his eight hundred and we counted the rest. It came to $24,900 and we split it down the middle. It wasn't what we'd expected when we'd gone into the crap-job but it was more than I thought we'd end up with during those first minutes in the barn.

"Payment before the job's over, huh?" Hump said, stuffing his share into his coat pocket.

"The job we were doing for Annie's over. Edwin's safe in jail by now." I went over to the junk drawer next to the sink. I found an old pair of scissors. "Help with this."

Hump cut the black driving glove away. "Charleston will be there tomorrow afternoon."

"If he's the stud Francine says he is," I said.

"Francine...shit. She's over at my place." But he took his time and worked the glove off my left hand. It was sore and stiff but the bandage still covered it to some degree.

"I'll drive you over to pick up your car."

On the drive Hump said, "Charleston's yours, but I'll back you."

"Appreciate that," I said.

After I left Hump I stopped off at a pay phone and called Annie Murton. I told her where Edwin was and that she could probably go over and see him right away. If she'd ask for Art he'd fix up a visit for her. She thanked me but it didn't seem like her heart was in it. I think she was already running ahead, thinking about her visit to Edwin. I could understand that and it wasn't anything I'd complain about.

It was a deep dreamless sleep until around seven, first light. I awoke then but I still felt tired and I tried to force it. It was then I had the dreams, dreams about people with white bloodless slashes at their throats like fish gills. So finally I said to hell with it and got up. I made coffee and got the *Constitution* from the doorstep and read the sports page. I listened to the radio and it was all about it never raining in California and how this one guy was meeting Mrs. Jones at the same café everyday. It might have been more fun if they'd met at a motel. And when I'd had enough of sports and the music, I shut my mind to it and thought about Charleston.

At seven the blond young man came out of a stand of pines fifteen miles away from the Dairy. His clothes were somewhat rumpled but he didn't look like a road barn. The second car he thumbed stopped for him. It was a green Toyota driven by a young construction worker on his way to his job on the complex at Colony Square. He rode that far and thanked the man and walked down half a block to a cafe and had breakfast.

The job wasn't over, he knew that. Those four kids were out there somewhere, running scared. But the priority had changed since last night. Even if it was free, if he didn't get a dime for it, the fat man was next. Even if he blew the whole job because of it. And that was a promise he made himself.

After he had his second cup of coffee he walked a few blocks up Peachtree until he reached 10th. There didn't seem to be any cabs around so he caught a # 10 bus and rode it downtown.

⚜ ⚜ ⚜

The phone rang around eleven and I caught it on the third ring. I assumed that it was Hump. Instead it was a masculine-voiced woman who said it was Western Union and she had a telegram for Mr. James Hardman.

"Read it," I said.

"Are you Mr. Hardman?" she asked.

"Unless you've got a wrong number."

"This is your telegram: *Arriving on the eight-ten tonight. Meet me if you like. Do not if it is too much trouble.* The telegram is signed 'Marcy.'"

It sounded like her and it sounded like she hadn't gotten over the burn from the night she'd called.

"Would you like me to repeat the message?" the woman asked.

"No," I said, "once is enough."

At twelve I got out the card Connie had given me at the breakfast-and-lunch place on Bricker Road, the one with only a phone number on it. I dialed the number. A woman answered. It wasn't a voice I'd have matched with the blonde, Connie, but I asked it anyway. "Connie?"

"Yes."

"This is Al Burns. I was there yesterday. Remember me?"

"Yes, Al."

"About what I was talking about. I talked to my poker friends and they're interested."

"I hope you realize that the fee for such a party would be quite expensive, Al."

"How much?" I asked.

"One thousand," Connie said.

"That's steep," I said, "but I've got my quarterly bonus socked away."

"Then I believe we can set a firm date," she said.

"Tonight, I want tonight."

"I'm afraid that's not possible. I checked my engagement calendar and I find we already have plans today."

"Aw, hell," I said.

"Tomorrow is open," she said.

"I'd rather have today," I said, "but if it's taken...."

"Tomorrow then." Then she said if I wanted the evening kept for me I'd have to drop by a deposit of five hundred before noon the following day.

I said I would. That I'd send my driver, Horace, by.

"See you then, Al."

"I'm looking forward to it," I said.

But today, I thought, as I broke the connection.

CHAPTER FOURTEEN

From around one to two Hump and I had lunch at the White Horse in Underground Atlanta. It was mainly a roast beef place and we both had a couple of ribs worth of the rare. We kept the drinking down. It wasn't anything we talked about. Maybe we read each other's minds.

Hump dropped me at the doctor's office so I could get the hand checked and the bandage changed. He'd said he'd be right back, that he had an errand.

Hump was parked in the lot, waiting for me when I came out. There was a flat thick object in a brown paper bag on the seat next to him. He didn't explain what it was and I didn't ask. It didn't seem the right size for anything that would fire silver bullets.

We drove around for a while and picked up Art at exactly four. When Art got into the front seat with us, Hump lifted the brown paper bag and tossed it into the back seat. It hit there with a heavy thud.

"Good to have your money back?"

"Great," Hump said.

While Hump was answering, Art had turned to watch my face.

On the drive to the department Art filled us in on what he'd picked out of the boys during the late-night questioning. The original plan had been Jake's. When he met Edwin and saw how much the kid needed money to attract Heddy, he'd turned the kid to his uses. Heddy had helped in that. One night in bed and the promise of many more to come. Edwin had enlisted the other four from the Burger Shack. The only loose end had been tied up, too. On the night of the robbery, Fred Maxwell had been the one outside the house on the walkie-talkie, the guy who'd counted the guests as they approached the house and alerted the guys inside. It looked like Jake had trusted the kids or he had trusted Edwin's passion for Heddy. The split was to be made the night Jake was killed and Edwin and the others had driven over to Jake's Headhunter Lounge and found the lot full of police cars. After that they'd stayed at the Dairy. Not leaving it, waiting to see if anyone would come looking for thorn. Of course they heard about the death of Jake but they weren't sure it was connected with the robbery. It just meant they were a lot richer.

"Why use kids?" I asked. "I always thought Jake had some sense."

"They didn't know. My guess is Jake knew no pro would take on a job like that. It had to be the innocents or nobody."

The night before, they'd been in the tobacco barn cleaning some of the grass and Henry Harper had said he was hungry, that he was going back to the main house for something to eat. Charleston must have messed up there because they'd heard one scream out of him and they'd had enough sense not to go out and look for him. Maybe they'd been expecting it. They'd gone out the back window and cut into the woods. They were afraid to try to reach the van so they'd tried for the highway.

"It was still a good piece of work," Hump said, "until the hounds got there."

"Any charges on the boys yet?"

"The D.A.'s working on that now. There's breaking and entering at the Rosewood Circle house. And if we can convince a few good citizens to step forward and testify, we might tag them with armed robbery." Art leaned across me and stared at Hump. "How about you as a witness?"

"Not likely."

"A good citizen, huh?"

"Just getting by," Hump said. "As far as I'm concerned, they took their chances and the pros among them got caught. The kids can do some probation or some time in one of the youthful offender camps. Other than that I'll draw the line at the bottom and say that part is over."

"I'm with Hump on that," I said.

"Should have known better than to have asked."

Hump parked in a lot down the street and we walked over to the department. On the chance that Charleston might know my car and Hump's, we'd decided to use-Art's unmarked car. That had the added advantage of a police radio if it went wrong somehow.

Art came out and we got in his car and headed for Bricker Road. We were still ahead of the time schedule I'd worked out. A few blocks from the Bricker Road place, Art checked his watch and pulled over and parked. He got a folded sheet of paper out of his jacket pocket and spread it on the dashboard. "Before I left last night I had the day squad get the word to check out the area for us. I wanted a rundown on the houses around, who lived there, drives, backyards, and so forth." He tapped his finger on a block that represented the house on the other side of 1122. "Think our best bet is to work from here. There's a hedge fence between but the drive is high and from what the day man said you can sit in a car in the drive and see the road and see the driveway of 1122. That is, we can see any car approaching on the road and we can see who gets out of the car in the driveway."

"That's one-sided," I said.

"You're right. It might be better to bracket it, use houses on both sides, cut off any possible escape route. The thing is—I don't want to run the risk that too much activity might be noticed." He shook his head. "No, we can't chance that. I think we can get him just using three sides."

"Tell it to us," I said.

He had it worked out so that I'd be in the car in the driveway on the other side of 1122, the car turned and pointing out to the road. Hump would be far up the driveway behind the car, at the fence looking over into 1122. He'd keep an eye on me. Art would get through the hedge and set up at the corner of the house nearest the hedge. As soon as the last customers left ... that would be around five ... we'd set up for the next car to approach the house. "When you see it you start the engine. That's my signal if I don't see him. As soon as he enters the drive you leave the driveway and pull in behind him, blocking that way out." Art looked at Hump. "As soon as Hardman pulls out of the drive, that's your cue to go over the fence and cover the backyard, just in case he gets away from us and heads in that direction."

"Looks good," Hump said.

"Only one thing," I said. "You drive the car and I go through the hedge."

"With that bad hand?"

"You want me to get arrested for driving police property?"

"How do you stand on this?" Art asked Hump. "It's trouble for you if he can't hack it."

"He can hack it," Hump said.

And that was that.

Hump and I waited in the driveway next to 1122 while Art went in. He was inside for around fifteen minutes. When he came out I saw a lace curtain pulled aside at one of the front windows and two withered and tiny little faces peered out at us. They were both topped with mounds of gray hair so I assumed they were ladies. Art got in the car and started it up. "That really made their day," Art said. "Both ladies are about eighty and spinsters and I had a hell of a time trying to find the right word for cathouse, something I could say to them. So I said bordello and that was almost as shocking to them as whorehouse."

He pulled into the road and turned and backed up the drive. "I had to tell them something so I said we were going to raid this bordello next door."

"I hope they don't come out to watch."

"I warned them against that. Said they could get arrested if they got in the way."

We settled down to wait. Now and then the lace curtain would curl away and the small faces would appear, remain for a brief moment and vanish as the curtain swung down again.

A few minutes before five the trickle from 1122 Bricker Road began. In ones and twos the men left, coming out and crossing the driveway to their cars. That was when the road race started. They'd pull out of there like a race start, as if they wanted to get as far away from the house as they could in as short time as they could. After that, they could always act like they were coming from somewhere else. Even before the last customer left, Francine came out, still in her maid's uniform and a raincoat, and backed a VW out of the garage.

"There's your girl," I said.

"That mean it's off?" Art asked.

"Still in costume," I said. "Might be an errand."

"Booze or some dope's my guess," Hump said.

"Time," I said. I got out of my topcoat and passed it back to Art. Hump got out and nodded and moved down the driveway toward the low fence that separated the house of the two old ladies and 1122. I bent down and checked the hedge, looking for a break. I found one finally, a low opening where the neighborhood dogs must have tunneled. I got to my knees and crawled into it. It was hard with the one hand and it seemed to be taking hours. When I was almost through I snagged my pants and it was a job to kick myself free. For a frightening moment there I could see myself having to face Charleston from that position and it wasn't something I liked.

I made a low run for the corner of the house. I squatted there and tried to even my breath. I couldn't see Art from my low angle and if a hitch came up I didn't know how I'd get his attention. I looked around and found two or three smooth stones. With my luck, if I had to toss one I'd end up paying for a windshield.

I settled down for the wait. One man came out and drove away and then another. Unless there was a customer who'd left his car out on the street, that did it. The house was empty except for the girls. Now we didn't have to worry about a customer walking into the middle of a shoot-out.

Ten minutes went by and then another ten. And then a suspicion jumped up at me. Had someone in 1122 seen the activity in the driveway and sent Francine out to warn Charleston? To meet him down the road and turn him back? I threw that around for a few minutes and didn't buy it. There wasn't any way for the girls to know why or that we were interested in Charleston. Any activity could mean, to them, that a vice raid was coming. And yet, none of the girls had left the house. So, no warning.

And then, as if to bear me out, I heard the rough engine of the VW. It was Francine. On the other side of the hedge I heard Art kick the engine over and then, immediately, shut it down. But then it caught again and I turned toward the hedge and when I turned back I saw the dark blue Capri turn into the driveway. The VW continued on into the garage and out of sight. Oh, shit, Francine, please stay in the garage ... just a minute longer. But even as I whispered that to myself she came around the corner of the house. Charleston ... I could see the blond hair ... was still in the car, unbuckling his seat belt. All right, I thought, then go straight into the house.

She didn't do that, either. She stopped and moved a few paces toward Charleston's car. Waiting for him, it seemed. I brought up the .38 and tried to line it up on him. He opened the door and stepped out and slammed the door behind him. I didn't have a shot. She was within the line and I relaxed. Maybe when he reached her he'd clear himself and I'd have a better angle. At that moment Art left the driveway on the other side of the hedge and Charleston looked up, startled for just a moment, and then reached Francine and said something and laughed and put an arm around her waist. He was too close. Move away from him, back away. Even as she pushed him away and he grabbed at her, Art turned up the driveway. He skidded and fishtailed. I took my eyes off Charleston for an instant and when I turned back he was straightening up, his pants leg high on one side. There was a flash in his hand and he had a knife against Francine's neck. The other hand caught her high in the chest and turned her, putting her between himself and Art who was out of the car and moving toward him.

"Police," Art said, "hands on your head."

"Don't take another step," Charleston said, "or I'll bleed her right here."

Then he moved a step backwards. Then another step. That was it, he was going to try to make it up to the porch and into the house. I could drop him anytime I wanted to but I'd take all or part of Francine with him. That went against my promise to The Man and I wasn't sure that Hump would care much for it either.

"Drop the knife and step away from her," Art yelled at him.

Charleston continued to move toward the steps. A step back and then a jerk at Francine that pulled her against his chest. I watched his shuffle. One step and a pull. Another step and a pull. He was close to the first step but he hadn't looked back yet. That might be the chance. I saw him reach back the leg, higher now, and feel for the step. The leg was far back and I could see driveway beyond the leg. It wasn't a high percentage shot. It was the only one I might get. I steadied the .38 over my left forearm, got the leg in the sights and squeezed off two rounds. One or both hit him. It was like somebody had kicked the other leg from under him. He whirled away from Francine and the knife kicked up into the air and landed several feet away.

Francine didn't know where to move. She made a lunge toward me and saw the gun and changed her mind. Art was coming at a run and that unnerved her even more. The third choice rounded the far corner of the house and she gave a cry and ran toward Hump.

I moved over and looked down at Charleston. He was curled in a ball, both hands gripping his left knee. Blood was running through his fingers. He was gasping and his lips were pulled back against his teeth, pale and bloodless.

Art joined me and I handed him the .38 and straightened Charleston out and patted him down from his neck to his shoes. All I found was the empty sheath.

The front door opened and Connie looked out. Behind her were two of her girls. One of the girls was Melba.

"Police," Art said to them.

Charleston was in some pain now, but his eyes were clear and dry. He looked hard enough to take the pain. He licked at his lips. "You're Hardman, I guess."

I held up the bandaged hand. "I thought you'd recognize your initials."

"Luck," he said, looking at the hand.

Art looked at the blood welling out of the wound. It was darkening the driveway under the leg and soaking the length of the pants leg. Art snaked his belt off and wrapped it around Charleston's leg above the knee. When he put pressure on it, Charleston winced and bit his lip.

"Bad luck got me," Charleston said.

I hooked a thumb at the three whores in the doorway. "If that's what you want to call them."

He tried to grin then. "Joker," he said, "you're some joker."

Closer now, with the grace and the deadliness gone, he looked like any number of those young men who seemed to remain eternally young for years and then overnight they grew old. That would happen to him. With the knee torn up, if he knifed anyone else he'd have to hire somebody to hold them for him. And when his business was death you could write him off as out of business.

"Hey … you … cop." It was one of the girls in the doorway calling. I didn't look up because I didn't think of myself as a cop anymore.

"You … the fat cop."

I looked up at the girl. It was Melba. It would take too long to explain that I wasn't a cop, so I answered, "Yeah?"

"You want some more head?"

Shrieking, laughing, the three whores backed into the house and slammed the door behind them with a loud smack.

Hump and I left before the ambulance or the other patrol cars arrived. Art had his spare .38 back and he had Charleston. Now if there was just something he could charge Charleston with. There was the assault on me at Maxwell's place and Hump would have to lie a little to hang that on him. That is, he'd have to testify he'd got a full face look at Charleston that afternoon he'd limped down from the breezeway between apartments 14 and 16. With Francine's help we might tag him with another assault charge. But there were other deaths, the deaths of Jake, of Heddy, the old actor, and the Harper kid that we'd have a hard time placing at Charleston's doorstep. Art, of course, would try to talk to Beck as soon as Beck could talk. That was a long chance. Beck was busted up and he might not be the man he once was. Still, there wasn't any reason to believe he was so far gone that he'd spill his guts in a courtroom. Beck was too much an organization man for that.

With Charleston down, Art was easy to get along with. Hump took him aside and said that Francine was a special friend and she'd helped us and couldn't he sort of forget about her when the vice squad came out to do their bust?

"Anyway," I said, "we need a ride into town." That might have been what pushed it over toward yes. I don't think Art wanted us around when the rest of the cops got there. He had enough to explain already.

On the way into town in Francine's little VW, we passed an ambulance making a hell of a racket and a couple of police cars tearing the late afternoon traffic into shreds. Hump drove us over to the lot where he'd left his car and I left them alone for a few minutes while they made whatever plans they had to make. I didn't hear it but I saw him take out his roll and peel off some bills. While she put those in her purse, he worked a key I took to be his apartment key off his ring and handed that to her. He kissed her and put her into the car and waved her out of the lot.

We waited for the parking lot attendant to work his car out of a block. Hump said, "I've got this idea. Why don't I go out to the airport with you and meet Marcy?"

That seemed friendly enough. He knew, from what I'd told him, that Marcy was pissed at me. Maybe he felt that he could act as a buffer until Marcy calmed down some.

"Then I thought I'd take you two and my new girl out to supper."

I had a feeling he was cooking something, that it was boiling and bubbling in him. "Any special place you want this supper?"

"The Gondola," Hump said.

The meeting with Marcy was stiff at first. I think she felt I'd be tight and distant and she'd backed away into herself. When I lifted her and kissed her hard and hungry, she had a hard time coming out again.

Hump stood in the background, grinning to himself. As soon as I released Marcy, he stepped forward and winked at her and got her tickets. He went to pick up her bags.

I put an arm around her and said, "Look, Marcy, it's over, it's done. The only damage is to my hand. The rest of me is whole." I leaned over and kissed on the soft line of her jaw. "And I did miss you, badass."

She turned then and I could see the crow marks around her eyes and. the blink of moisture and I knew it was all right.

"We got time for a drink or are we in a hurry?" I asked when Hump came back with the bags.

"No hurry. My girl's out at one of those malls trying to find some place to buy her some uptown threads."

"Is this a new girl?" Marcy asked. She liked Hump a hell of a lot and she always had an interest in the string of girls that Hump ran by for inspection from time to time.

"A young virgin Hump saved from ritual sacrifice," I said.

"With Jim's help," Hump said.

"And from the slam as well."

"That too," Hump said.

Marcy looked from one of us to the other, that puzzled look on her face and we went out to look for the drinks. We could tell her then as much as we wanted her to know.

Francine looked like about half a million dollars when we picked her up at Hump's apartment a little before ten. She'd bought herself a gray tweed pants suit and some of those god-awful thick-soled shoes that made most women walk like they were club-footed. On her they didn't seem to spoil the grace.

We reached The Gondola parking lot around ten. Hump remained behind a second to lock the car and when he caught up with us, he was carrying the brown paper bag with the thick bulky object in it. He saw me give it a hard look. He didn't explain and I didn't ask. I decided to wait and let this grown-up man do what he wanted to.

The maître d' remembered us and he wanted to lead us into the main dining room. It was Hump's party and he was in the lead. He shook his head at the maître d' and pointed at the table we'd had a couple of nights before. Jocko was back at his usual booth and I saw him give us a brief look and then dip his head.

The maître d' didn't like it much. He turned and looked in the direction of Jocko. He wanted help but Jocko didn't seem to want to give him any. All this hesitation irritated Hump and he took Francine's arm and pushed past the maître d' and headed for the table. Marcy didn't understand any of this and she gave me a worried look. I shook my head at her and took her arm and followed Hump and Francine. The maître d', with nothing better to do, brought up the rear.

We sipped at the first drinks. Hump still didn't indicate exactly what he had in mind. He was chatting along with Francine and Marcy and didn't act at all like a man about to do anything rash. The talk wandered for a few more minutes. I'd about decided that Hump didn't intend anything except to drop by and let our live bodies speak for us when Hump turned from Francine and dropped an eyelid at me. "What say we pay our respects to Mr. Giacommo?"

"Fine with me," I said. "Now?"

"Why not?"

Marcy looked up at me. "Is that nice Mr. Giacommo here?"

I leaned over to her. "Explanation later, but he's really not that nice. Keep Francine company."

Before we left the table Hump stripped the bag away and I saw that he had an up-to-date Sears Roebuck catalogue. I saw the direction then but I didn't say anything. We crossed the aisle and stood next to Jocko's table, waiting for him to look up. He kept us waiting too long and Hump held the catalogue about three feet above the booth table and dropped it. That got Jocko's attention.

"Ah, Mr. Evans and Mr. Hardman. Back so soon?"

"I like the way you fix spaghetti and meatballs," Hump said. "About as good as a spade place over on Boulevard."

Jocko gave us his good-host smile but Hump pushed a stony stare back at him. What the hell, Hump was my friend, so I matched the stone in his.

Jocko tapped the Sears Roebuck catalogue with a manicured nail. "What's this?"

"I thought you'd remember. I told you if you ever turned Beck loose on me you'd have to order another one. Well, you can order now, but try to get a better one. He wasn't good enough."

"I heard," Jocko said unruffled, "that George had an accident."

"That wasn't any accident," Hump said. "That was on purpose."

The good-host smile vanished. "Is there anything else, gentlemen?"

"One thing more," Hump said. "You tell him Jim."

"Since you're going to order anyway," I said, "you might as well order me a new playmate, too. The last one didn't wear very well. I shot him in the knee this afternoon and made him a charity case."

That puzzled him. I guess he hadn't heard about Charleston yet. "Which playmate was that?"

"Charleston."

He paled on that. "Where?"

"In front of a whorehouse."

He thought about that for a few seconds. "It's been nice talking to you, gentlemen, but as you can see I'm very busy...."

"Write it off," I said. "Close the contract down. It's over and you know it. Jake's dead, the dancer's dead, one of the kids is dead, Maxwell's probably dead though we haven't found the body yet...and some poor old guy who wasn't involved is dead. Of the eight involved in the rip-off, four are dead. Call it half a warning and write it off."

"I never take business advice from strangers," Jocko said.

When Hump and Francine left my house, it was well after one a.m. and there was a cold, brittle rain falling, a rain that might turn into sleet if the temperature continued to drop. It was the first time Marcy and I had been alone since I'd met her at the airport and I could feel the stiffness creeping back between us.

"Bedtime," I said.

I left her in the kitchen straightening up and went into the bathroom and washed up and brushed my shaky old teeth. I left the light on in the bathroom and cut out the bedroom lights. I undressed and got into bed and waited.

Marcy went by without speaking and I doubled the pillow behind my head and listened to the tap of the cold rain until the roar of the shower drowned it out. When the shower stopped I could hear the wind blowing the rain against the windows. And waited. And waited. Trying to tell from the sounds in the bathroom exactly what she was doing. That's a way of passing the time. Hard time.

When she finally came out of the bathroom she was wearing my old terrycloth robe and from the light in the bathroom I could see a few drops of water on her forehead and a soggy strand or two of hair in the back. She sat on the edge of the bed, turned toward me, facing me but not close.

"Something's changed in you. I don't know what it is yet. But...since a woman always thinks it's just one thing...I'll ask that one question. Have there been any girls in my bed while I was in Fort Myers?"

"One," I said and then that line out of Marlowe floated up out of nowhere, out of some night course at Georgia State. "But that was in another country and besides the wench is dead."

"Tell me about it, Jim." She was calm and that wasn't at all like her.

I told her about Heddy, the whole story, waking up in the bed and finding her there. Heddy's gift that wasn't a gift but a bribe and how I couldn't take it. And death face down in a ditch. At the end she kicked off my shower shoes and stretched out on the bed beside me. I shifted over to make room for us and straightened out the pillow and offered her part of it.

"And all that's the truth?" she asked.

"Yes."

I waited but it wasn't a long wait. Marcy turned and put an arm across my chest and pressed against me. "Maybe there's hope for you yet, Jim. Maybe you aren't so hard-assed after all."

And after a time we slept the sleep of good, kind lovers.

ABOUT THE AUTHOR

R alph Dennis isn't a household name ... but he should be. He is widely considered among crime writers to be a master of the genre, denied the recognition he deserved because his twelve *Hardman* books, which are beloved and highly sought-after collectables now, were poorly packaged in the 1970s by Popular Library as a cheap men's action-adventure paperbacks with numbered titles.

Even so, some top critics saw past the cheesy covers and noticed that he was producing work as good as John D. MacDonald, Raymond Chandler, Chester Himes, Dashiell Hammett, and Ross MacDonald.

The *New York Times* praised the *Hardman* novels for "expert writing, plotting, and an unusual degree of sensitivity. Dennis has mastered the genre and supplied top entertainment." The *Philadelphia Daily News* proclaimed *Hardman* "the best series around, but they've got such terrible covers..."

Unfortunately, Popular Library didn't take the hint and continued to present the series like hack work, dooming the novels to a short shelf-life and obscurity...except among generations of crime writers, like novelist Joe R. Lansdale (the *Hap & Leonard* series) and screenwriter Shane Black (the *Lethal Weapon* movies), who've kept Dennis' legacy alive through word-of-mouth and by acknowledging his influence on their stellar work.

Ralph Dennis wrote three other novels that were published outside of the *Hardman* series—*Atlanta, Deadman's Game* and

MacTaggart's War—but he wasn't able to reach the wide audience, or gain the critical acclaim, that he deserved during his lifetime.

He was born in 1931 in Sumter, South Carolina, and received a masters degree from University of North Carolina, where he later taught film and television writing after serving a stint in the Navy. At the time of his death in 1988, he was working at a bookstore in Atlanta and had a file cabinet full of unpublished novels.

Brash Books will be releasing the entire *Hardman* series, his three other published novels, and his long-lost manuscripts.